MW01128503

A Musician's Story

By

John Charles Unger

Bloomington, IN

Milton Keynes, UK

AuthorHouse™
1663 Liberty Drive, Suite 200
Bloomington, IN 47403
www.authorhouse.com
Phone: 1-800-839-8640

AuthorHouse™ UK Ltd.
500 Avebury Boulevard
Central Milton Keynes, MK9 2BE
www.authorhouse.co.uk
Phone: 08001974150

First published by AuthorHouse 3/2/2006

ISBN: 1-4259-1555-8 (sc)

Library of Congress Control Number: 2006900497

Printed in the United States of America
Bloomington, Indiana

This book is printed on acid-free paper.

Dedicated to the two bravest people I ever knew, Frank and Agnes Unger, (I miss you guys every day;) my kids, Michael, Jason, and Julia; Dale; Frances and Steve; Mom- Sal, (where would I be without you) Roberta, for editing so beautifully, and last but certainly not least, my California pal, Richie.

For All My Friends and Family

A Musician's Story

As I performed 'Unchained Melody' for the umpteenth time in my thirty-five year career, the three, sixty-something's that had camped in front of me all night getting totally wasted, gradually oozed out of their seats and staggered to the dance floor. There, they formed a kind of friendship circle, a man and two women, he trying to lead and they, not following exactly. Finally a side-to-side motion was agreed upon and soon the swaying went too far and down they all went into a heap, ladies' dresses coming up over their waists! Had it not looked so funny, it might have been sad. I couldn't even finish my song.

"If you guys are driving tonight, give me a 10-minute head start," came out of my mouth, as I tried to regain composure. The Dandy's crowd, by this time of night nothing but a bunch of drunks themselves, howled with laughter. I couldn't help it. I knew these three people, and I had never in a million years pictured them, upside down. But one of the gals that fell was not amused.

"You embarrassed us that night with your comment," the ex-teacher with far too much lipstick finally spoke to me two weeks later. How about your own behavior, any embarrassment about that? I wanted to scream but held my tongue. For Pete's sake, enough was enough; God how I wanted to be in Florida! Frustration at my lack of career was making me crazy. I was fifty and still playing dives

in Michigan. On stage I'd function automatically, but in my mind, to keep from going completely insane I'd retreat to a simpler, more innocent time. This is my story.

Chapter One

"Catch a falling star and put it in your pocket,

Save it for a rainy day..."

-Perry Como

1950

When I think about it now, it was a wonderful way to start life. Frank and Agnes David already had their seven-year-old birth daughter Frances, and for whatever blessed reason, they felt compelled to adopt a son. They named me John Charles. What a lucky break for me. After all, I could just as easily have been adopted by alcoholic kid-torturers! But instead I got the two best parents on Earth and an entire Mennonite community and culture to grow up in. It was fabulous!

My adoptive blue-eyed dad was a hard-working, physical man. As a sharecropper farmer he slaved in the stifling tobacco kilns of Southern Ontario from sunrise to sunset. In the evenings he would return to our happy household and still wearing his soiled muscle shirt, he'd hold me high in the air, his strong arms gently lowering me back down to my soft bed. He'd make my mother, sister, and I giggle with his antics.

He was and will always be my hero.

Then there was my mom, the slim and pretty Agnes. She was the one that named me Charles after England's famous Prince. She was slim with model-good-looks but the integrity of a nun. A terrific homemaker, the focal point of the David family's entire existence was her busy kitchen. Her dog-eared Mennonite cookbook held recipes for sweet, luscious baked goods like Zwieback and Razinen-Schtruetzel, and every Saturday afternoon, my 4-year-old neighborhood pals and I would wait patiently at the back door for those hot, delicious samples. It was a weekly ritual we couldn't have done without.

Frances was right out of the Big Sister Book. Tall and slender with long, reddish brown curly hair and lots of freckles, she could have been resentful of me, the one suddenly getting all the attention, but instead was gentle and protective. Our whole lives, every holiday she and I would reminisce about the time as a 3-year-old I wandered away from her watchful babysitting eyes and became lost in a freak snowstorm in the vast open acreage a mile behind our house.

In the blistering wind and whipping snow of a real Canadian blaster my ten-year-old sister had the courage and determination to follow my footprints and find me by the railway tracks. She wrapped her arms around me,

"Oh thank God you're safe, don't ever run away again," she exclaimed giving me her earmuffs, her frozen hands cupped around my face.

I was *so* glad to see her. Until we were adults we never revealed to our folks what had happened that day, and then only in passing, at Thanksgiving dinner.

"Remember the day Johnny got lost in the back yard?" Throughout my life, she would always have my back, and I hers.

It was a Mennonite community all right, not as strict as the Amish but still very straight-laced. There were no beards or dark clothing, by appearances the Mennonites in our town looked like everybody else. Nevertheless they had the beard-and-dark-clothing attitude. But wait a minute. They were supposed to have nothing and live like paupers weren't they? The parking lot at our church was always filled with brand new cars every Sunday morning and the farmers in our community always had the latest and newest equipment to harvest their crops. They didn't believe in keeping their talents under a bushel.

The Mennonites were some of the best farmers on earth. Some of them were so good at it that their work year was only six months and the other six months were spent in Florida! But the half-year spent in Ontario was definitely hard labor. I had school friends who literally disappeared for a time during harvesting months. The only time I saw them was in Sunday service and many times they went directly from there, to the fields.

"See ya later," I'd wish them on the steps of our church knowing full well I wouldn't.

Any Mennonite farmer that grew tomatoes for the H. J. Heinz factory in Leamington knew that nothing less than an "A" rating would do. The hard hot picking was just the beginning. Then there was the careful loading so as not to damage even one of the smooth succulent fruits. Then there was waiting in line, sometimes all night with his precious cargo, to unload and get his score.

Clearly I remember the day Mr. Taves came roaring down the lane as we picked in the hot sun, his shrieks of joy heard above the noise of his tractor pulling the loose, chuckling empty wagons.

"We got an A! We got an A!" He shared it with us as though it was our farm and our field. And it was. We were all so thrilled.

My mother too had a sense of the land and what it could produce. Forever, I will remember the sharp canning smells emanating from her kitchen during the hot days of summer. We helped in a beehive of activity, stuffing crisp and crunchy cucumbers, sun-drenched tomatoes, or explosively sweet peaches in glass jars, pouring hot wax on top and sealing them quickly shut.

"I'll bet you're glad now, aren't you Johnny?" my dear Mom would tease in the bitter cold of February, as she handed me a slice of warm, homemade bread topped with melting butter and fresh strawberries. Oh yeah I was.

Because life in Leamington was rooted in the earth, my childhood years came right out of a storybook. I climbed trees, swam in ponds, rode horses, and did most of it without adult supervision. My 5-year-old world rivaled Disneyland! C H I R, the local 5000 watt AM station, played the hits of the fifties in between farm reports on our white GE radio. Thanks to my mom, that radio was *always* on.

Our creaky wooden sharecropper house had no electricity of its own but was supplied by a rather long extension cord that stretched across the yard to the boss-man's house. That worked fine unless too many things were turned on at one time which for my grumbling father would mean trudging to the neighbors and replacing the fuse. There was also no plumbing.

Anyone who has ever used a portable 'John' has some idea of what our outhouse must have looked, smelled, and felt like. It was cold; in winter it was desperation-only, and it was real life. I'll never forget it. My father would have given a frozen testicle for a Home Depot! Bathing meant saving rainwater in a barrel and boiling it. The last bather, which was usually my Dad, was really using everybody else's water. Funny, he never complained, at least not that I remember. But I'm sure he must have. How could you not?

Old Mr. Taves, the Mennonite farmer we sharecropped for, was another one of my heroes. He would drive his giant tractors all day long on the hundreds of acres that rolled behind our house. Despite the fact he was our landlord, he was as kind and gentle a man as ever lived. I'd hear his grumbling diesel chugging down the bumpy lane and dash excitedly outside, screen door squeaking and closing lazily behind me, to open the gate for him.

"At-a-boy Johnny," the man in the engineer's hat would holler down to me over the roar of the diesel engine. Any 5-year-old would be totally jazzed! From atop that huge John Deere, Uncle Jack, as our family would call him even though he was not a real uncle, would shoot snot out of one nostril at a time with incredible intensity and accuracy. He would do this while I ran with the gate. What was amazing to me was the string attached.

"Thank you!" he waved at me as he drove through, the tractor noise breaking the spell.

Life went on like that day after day, in an endless chain of happy experiences, with only the occasional exception. Back in '57, my neighborhood pal Bobby Conrad and I had the brilliant idea of selling tomatoes by the roadside. It was August and each of us, being only 7 at the time, failed to realize that in a farming community, tomatoes were in over-abundance and not likely to be desired by the folks speeding by. In our county, they grew tomatoes on the front porch, back porch, side porch, front yard, back yard, and every nook that held a planter. Everyone had more than they could use. It was the tomato capital of Canada for Pete's sake. H. J. Heinz was two miles away!

Our entrepreneurial waves and smiles soon turned to frustration and we developed a plan for those that would dare ignore us. We were supposedly aiming at the tires, but one perfectly thrown curveball, I won't divulge the pitcher's name, sliced neatly through the open side window and 'splatted' full-force into the side of a man's head. It must have been quite a shock that day.

One minute you're running just a little bit late for that cow auction and the next... a ripe, juicy tomato comes flyin' through yer winda. It knocked the hat right off his head! Our jaws dropped as the vehicle slid to a screeching halt, kicking up a cloud of dust from the gravel shoulder, and then from Bobby's lips, I heard for the first time in my life, the expression:

"Oh shit!"

We got into serious trouble and Bobby's mother blamed me because her "angel" would never have done such a thing of his own accord. In hindsight, she was probably right because I was then, and always would be, a great and encouraging audience for anyone willing to go out on the edge for the sake of a laugh. I got my hide tanned for that one and so did Bobby, and now that I look back, rightfully so.

When I was eight, my family took a first time train ride to Manitoba to visit relatives. It was an amazing journey in the Scenic-Cruiser through Northern Ontario's stark rock formations and stampeding wildlife. There, in a rustic farming town south of Winnipeg, I met my slightly older cousins, Hardy and Rudy, for the first time. They spat too and used the "f" word a lot although I had no idea what it meant.

To me, a skinny, awed, 8-year-old, three things would stand out about this trip: taking a horse and buggy far into the woods and camping out, looking at a Playboy for the first time by flashlight, and hearing those two country boys wail on their guitars! There was something earthy and magical about the whole thing, and the strange correlation between 'skin' and music would be forever stamped in my young mind.

For the rest of the year, I thought a lot about those bare-naked ladies, but all I talked about was getting a guitar. On Christmas morning I got my wish. And you would think that I'd have been happy but of all things, Frances got a violin! When I saw that strangely knurled, shining wooden instrument, I was spellbound. Maybe it was all the orchestral music we had listened to on the radio or maybe it was sibling rivalry but just holding it in my hands filled me with magical delight!

And so it turned out that after a year of lessons we found ourselves, my whole family and me, along with little old violin teacher Sister Margaret, driving the three hours to London, to the Conservatory Of Music's awards ceremonies. I had won a prize.

Along the way, like rabbits out of a hat, Mom would magically pull a meticulously packed lunch out of a giant wicker basket.

"Who wants egg salad? Who wants fried chicken?" she would gleefully ask, each exploding out of the fresh, white, homemade bread Mennonite mothers were famous for. My jolly music teacher would give my mother her much appreciated praise,

"Oh Agnes, you've been much blessed by the Lord," and Mom would blush.

"There are radishes, celery, and pickles," she'd exclaim. No one could pack a picnic lunch like my mom. She thought of *everything.*

Later at the event, I waited shyly behind the curtain to walk out on stage and accept my medal. I was supposed to be the next honoree but horror of horrors, the announcer mistakenly called out, "Kathy McDonald." I didn't know what to do but because the elderly Master of Ceremonies motioned frantically for me to come forward, I did.

So there I stood, nine-years-old, in front of eight hundred people, my parents and violin teacher on their once-in-a-lifetime trip, accepting Kathy's award.

"No, that's not me," I tried to whisper to the old fart.

"Off you go," he muttered, ignoring my plea. It was the first experience of what felt like having my pants down in public, but certainly would not be the last.

All the way home my father grumbled under his breath,

"You'd think they could have gotten the doggone names right! How darned hard was that to do?" Then he added his patented and now familiar,

"Good Grief." For my Dad, this was really swearing.

Sister Margaret alternated briskly between knitting and crossing herself in the back seat.

The only other time Dad might step a little out of character was on Sunday afternoons when we would go into town for an old fashioned visit with the Tiessen's. Cousins of my mother, they had kids around my age and while we played games in the kitchen, from the living room I'd overhear their father say to mine,

"How about a beer Frank?" We never had alcohol in our home and in my young mind I thought this made the Tiessen's more modern, more like people on television. I loved going there. My Dad was quite predictable and always gave the same response,

"No thanks, I've got tools to sharpen later...well maybe just one."

An hour later there'd be an empty six-pack of Molson's between them and they'd both be chain smoking Export A's, hollering at the small black and white TV screen, where Big Time Wrestling would be on, showing what I thought were some of the phoniest wrestling moves I'd ever seen. I couldn't believe grown men could be so completely fooled! Nevertheless my Dad would be right into it, standing up, red in the face exclaiming,

"Good grief 'ref! Can't you see he's got sand in his shorts? Aw c'mon! Good grief!" Sometimes they'd both be out of their chairs pointing a finger at the TV and yelling,

"Oh for Pete's sake! What, are you blind?" I noticed that my mother would be unusually quiet on those rides home

Chapter Two

"Oh my Darling, Oh my Darling, Oh my Darling Clementine..."

...Stephen Foster

1960

When I was 10, my parents bought their own home. We were coming up in the world. We now had indoor plumbing and electricity, and even a 13-inch black and white TV! Our new neighbors Otto and Mary were wonderful. Also of the same faith and a little younger than my folks, they were a fantastic loving couple and delightfully eccentric. He liked to tinker with tape recorders and she loved to sing and had a very lovely voice. Boy did this ever shape *my* life.

They allowed all the kids in the neighborhood to play in their basement on rainy days. Sometimes they'd chauffeur a carload of us to school saving us from a grueling, two-mile, against-the-wind bike ride. It was like living next door to Dickens' Fezziwigs. The first time I set foot in Mary's grand kitchen to taste her German baking and hear her husky soprano soaring above the room, I thought I had died and gone to heaven.

As I savored her homemade apple fritters, she would keep a cheery conversation going with Valentine, the family's shy cocker spaniel. Like a Broadway actress, the portly woman would bend down quietly near the unsuspecting dog's face and start softly, building to a crescendo, changing the accent of each word:

"**Moo**-cho, Valen-**tee**-no, Val-**en**-tay, **VALENTINE,"** she'd sing, and the helpless, bombarded animal would go into a wagging frenzy. Then Mary would cap it off with,

"S-T-O-O-O-O-P-I-I-I-D!"

The "stupid" would be loud, and sounded like a "ding-dong" at the end, with lots of vibrato.

The helpless pooch curled in its basket seemed to understand because it couldn't thump its tail any harder, and then it would expose its top layer of teeth, as if it were smiling, and this made us laugh so hard we were both in tears. What a wonderful friendship I had with this woman.

One rainy day, there was a new sound. I followed my ears and peeked cautiously around the corner where to my astonishment, Mary sat with an acoustic guitar on her lap playing chords 'Hawaiian-style' by moving a metal slide bar in her left hand along the neck of the instrument, while strumming rhythmically with her right, and singing along. I stood there transfixed.

To me, the bluesy, jangling sound of the metal-faced guitar, accompanied by her twangy, country voice singing 'Clementine,' nailed me to the floor. It conjured up so sweetly all of the memories of my cousins, sitting by the crackling fire in the woods on that fresh September night, harmonizing so beautifully. With me sitting at her feet, open-mouthed, Mary lovingly showed me what she was doing and I picked it up instantly, as though I had known it all along. She taught me every song she knew and soon I was teaching myself songs from the radio!

When I look back at that period of my life, music played almost constantly in my head. I was the adopted son of humble Mennonite parents who had chosen to buy a home in the middle of nowhere, next door to a woman I adored that sang, played the guitar, and encouraged me to do likewise. How lucky could I be?

But all was not so rosy...

One afternoon, I arrived home from school to find two ladies from our church I barely knew and Mary in our house. Their faces told me something was wrong. My mother was not there. They informed me in soothing tones that she had crossed the road to get the mail and had been hit by a car. At twelve, I immediately went into denial at this news. She would recover from those injuries but during her hospital stay something else was discovered; a new disease called Multiple Sclerosis.

I didn't know what M.S. was or how devastating its effects would be on our family, but I would certainly come to know. Emotionally, it would rattle my cage at the deepest level, causing me to question everything I had ever been taught about God, Truth, Being and Mercy.

Just a few years later as a longhaired, bearded, angry teenager, I would sit across our kitchen table from the stiff, white-collared minister that had been sent by the church to 'straighten' me out, bravely pointing a finger in his face and practically screaming at him,

"Bullshit! That's bullshit! Do you think it's actually possible to love a God that would let my poor mother lie in there, suffering helplessly, day after day, year after year?" Tears were in my eyes. Poor man. He only wanted to help but there were no answers for me then.

Chapter Three

"Hot town, summer in the city Back 'o my neck gettin' dirt and gritty..."

–The Lovin' Spoonful

1963

When I was thirteen my folks bought a modest two-story home in nearby Kingsville, a peaceful community on the shores of Lake Erie. Thirty-five hundred or so year-round residents lounged at the quiet, easy pace of this small Canadian town. This was a daring move for my conservative parents, moving further away from the Mennonite community, but I'm sure glad they did it.

What a lovely town Kingsville was. The Cleavers would have liked it there with its quaint, maple tree-lined boulevards always clean and well maintained. Some of the burg's streets led straight to the waterfront, where golden sandy beaches and picture-perfect sunsets held an irresistible attraction for Michiganders.

I soon learned that in the 1960s, most of the hundreds of cottages dotting our little shoreline were American owned. Only an hour's drive from Dearborn, it was a quick and easy getaway for the stressed out executive, autoworker, teacher or nurse. I would see them on their back porch, always a drink in hand, staring in awe as did I, at Lake Erie's vast and calming presence.

The first time I ran the half-mile from our new home down to Surfside Park and saw the magnificent view from the high hill above the shoreline, I knew without a doubt why the Americans were there. It took my breath away. As a teenager and even into my twenties, through all the joys of love found and sorrows of its loss, this bucolic scene would always embrace me.

My father worked 6 days a week, trying to get off early on Saturdays. Mum stayed home, struggling from walker to wheelchair, trying to raise me. My sister had gone off to nursing school as I began my teenage years. A feeling of alienation began in my life and I grew to love being alone in my room with my guitar. My mother hated the instrument. In her mind, all that could be played on it was rock music, and that was somehow linked to Satan himself.

But I loved it because it made such a full sound, and I could sing along, which I had also begun to enjoy. With the guitar, I entered another world that I thought no one understood with the exception of Mary, my two cousins, and the bands on the radio. I played for hours mimicking the records, and it didn't matter what kind of music it was. It never occurred to me at that time that one had to choose! I liked everything. So there I was; tall, skinny me, trying to be "cool."

But I *really* loved Brian Wilson's music. It made me think of sun and sea, and the kids from the States I knew, how cool they were and how much I dug them. In almost every way, during summers, Kingsville was like a little California town. The Americans had a certain type of 'wits-about-them' expression, a kind of confidence; an attitude that some Canadians perceived as arrogance but I didn't think so. Canucks didn't realize that any 'Yanks' they saw were on vacation and with them, it was simply about living large for a few days.

It was not uncommon to see folks from the States driving around our little town with a beer between their legs. It mattered little to them whether their vacation was two days or two months, they were going to party and that was that. And as they were fond of saying with regard to the local police,

"Barney can't be everywhere at once."

The Yanks also brought sex to our fair shores, much to my delight! They seemed to think and talk about it more, and were more preoccupied with getting it. But then, at 13, I had begun to think about it quite a bit too. Whatever 'it' was, my friends and I were crazy for it.

One of the best places for us to anticipate actual sightings was a large sandy public beach area known as Cedar Island. Cozy and unspoiled, it was typically Canadian-clean, beautiful and picturesque, with plenty of leafy-green shade trees over hot, white sand. In every way, despite being in the northern hemisphere, it was like a tropical isle. Luxurious Ohio boats from Sandusky would cross the lake and put in for the week at Malloy's Marina. Daddies would bring daughters.

"Skin" seemed to magically appear. On lazy summer days, my pals and I would be there in cutoffs and sandals. There was a huge jukebox in the island's little cafeteria, where we guys would hang around waiting for chicks to come in for take out food, ice cream, or cigarettes for their parents. We'd make sure something hot and funky was always playing as loudly as we could get away with. Clear as yesterday, I can still hear the cry of the screen door, the smell of grilling onions, and the outstanding sound of the 'box.' It would vibrate the benches of our booth whenever one of us punched up 'Good Lovin' or 'I've Been Lonely Too Long' by The Young Rascals or 'Midnight Hour' or 'Knock On Wood' by Wilson Pickett. Ooh, that was good stuff.

Across the checkered tile floor the songs would reverberate in deep, bass tones and to us fresh young males, it couldn't have sounded better. Staring out, my gaze would drift past my fidgeting buddies, focused on yet another sailboat cruising slowly through the channel, heading for its mooring. At first only the mast could be seen, floating like a mysterious spire until it rounded the bend. Then the whole boat would come into view, as the crying seagulls swirled off to greet the next one.

As evening approached, the sun was a red rubber ball in a distant marmalade sky and I thought: what a great life I have.

Chapter Four

"Everybody loves a clown, so why don't you,

'Cause clowns have feelings too..."

-Gary Lewis and the Playboys.

As a 13-year-old, I found the transition to Kingsville uncomfortable in the beginning. Not only was I making the leap from living in the country to living in town, but I was also starting high school in the fall. Adding to this stress, I had broken my wrist, high jumping on grade 8 Field Day, and felt like a do-fuss, with a big bulky plaster cast!

Making friends was never a problem for me, but here in this new town, without any contacts, it was kind of scary. Throughout that first week, from the safety of our front porch, I eagerly searched up and down the street, anxious to meet anyone my age. Finally I noticed some girls standing in front of the big white house down at the corner. As shy as I was, desperate times called for desperate measures. I took a deep breath and pedaled there, one-handed, on my bike. Looking back, I can truly say that summoning up the courage that day changed the course of my life, and in a most delightful way.

"Hi," I managed.

"Hi," the round, pretty girl with short, black hair answered.

"I'm John."

"I'm Sherry," she blushed. It was instant relief to have found someone who could give me the straight poop on what was going on around town. And she certainly had the lowdown. She must have been on the phone all day long to have as much information as she did; about who was cool; who was dating whom. I could only concentrate on that kind of conversation for a while and then my eyes would begin to glaze over. That still happens.

"Oh…you've got to meet Corey Wagner; he plays drums!" she exclaimed. What was that? Who plays drums?

"Well..." she corrected herself,

"He plays *a* drum." To me this was unbelievable! She said he lived only a few blocks away on Pearl street but the wires must have been buzzing that night because the next day, Wagner came around on his bike, making a dramatic, swerving, rubber-burning stop in front of me and the swooning girls. I wished right away that I could have the effect he had on the opposite sex. The nervous girls started giggling the moment they spotted him.

This new 13-year-old was handsome, tall and lean, with perfect, wavy blonde hair, marble-blue eyes, amazing freckles, and what seemed to be a remarkably smooth tongue.

"Yeah, my Dad and I race go-carts!" he casually stated, resting his freckled arms on the handlebars, having a spit and looking down at the ground. A few pointed questions later, he would reveal that they didn't exactly *race* them, but they did *have* one!

I liked Corey immediately. For the rest of my life, people who meant something to me would always remind me of some famous personality or movie star. Dressing in the coolest, newest style, my pal looked like a young Jeff Bridges, very confident and very witty. I was tall and skinny and felt anything but hip with my lumpy cast, but my new pal thought I was okay and we would 'hang' every single day for what remained of that summer!

There we sat on Wagner's screened front porch in the shade, while life carried on as usual on his quiet, tree-lined street with occasional cars, passers by, and warm summer sunshine. Bees went from flower to flower, ever conscious of the slowly rotating sprinkler. Three doors down, a lonely dog chained in the back yard would let out an occasional yelp.

I would illustrate, as best I could, despite my bulky handicap, what I knew on guitar while my new cohort would say, in a sincere whisper,

"This is so cool," while tapping out the rhythm on his "drum set," a single toy, red-shale snare drum. It amazed me, even thinking about it 35 years later, what a great groove he had gotten out of only two broken drumsticks that a drummer at a public school dance had given him; and a toy snare! To me, his beats were infectious.

We decided right then and there that we would start a band.

Fueled by this dream, we became inseparable and thanks to Corey, I learned all the fads of the day. I became aware of everything going on in the 13-year-old boy-world whereas before, I didn't really pay attention. Wagner seemed to know things that no one else knew, the gossip, the new bands, the latest dances, and who was going to be on Ed Sullivan on Sunday night.

For Pete's sake, he knew all the girl's names that danced on American Bandstand! I was dazzled and felt privileged just to be able to hang with a cool guy like my new friend. At home, if I played a rock tune on my guitar, my mother would try to stifle it.

"Shush, shush, shush, nicht das Johnny," she'd say briskly in her stern German, you're-forbidden-speak.

Here at the Wagner home, I was free!

By far though, our biggest bond was a shared love of The Beach Boys and Corey and I made a pact that we would some day meet them. When that glorious summer ended and high school began, I had a great new friend in Corey Wagner. Because of this friendship, my transition to Kingsville High was painless.

One thing I sincerely regret, however, was being an enthusiastic audience for my friend's pranks. He was a real character. Because he was good looking, he seemed to get away with teasing other kids and he was truly cruel, but God he was funny, and everyone seemed to let him slide. Sometimes even the people he made fun of had to laugh! Nobody was spared, cripples, retards; he was a master. Why, he was so damned funny to me, in my Mennonite upbringing, this would never be laughed at, I should be ashamed, yet I loved it.

And then there were these class clowns: Bucky, a gangly, goateed, Gilligan look-a-like, had a good-sized nose and pants that only reached the tops of his ankles. He was a nineteen-year-old ninth grader who had already been driving himself to school for three years! He wore the same clothes every day and never combed his hair, not that there was anything wrong with that. He was almost like a 'punk,' way before his time. And like the famous TV star he resembled, every once in a while, he would actually display a flash of brilliance and the entire class would turn in shock to gaze upon him; his eyes were always half closed.

We'd breathe a collective sigh of wonder at his ability to compute the correct answer, until we stopped to realize that this was his second time in just the ninth grade!

What was so funny about this guy was that he was so boastful, and that actually made us respect him.

"*I'm* Bucky, *I'm* the guy," and other egotistical rantings he'd say. We'd laugh.

"Be there, b*e* there, yeah!" You could hear him yelling in the poolroom uptown, from around the corner at the newspaper stand. He sure made believers out of Corey and me! Of course, we were totally impressed with anyone who could make us laugh.

Bucky's most daring feat involved Mrs. Walton, our matronly French teacher. Perhaps because of her age and serious demeanor, or her unwillingness to speak any English at all in class, the way French teachers tended to do, she had acquired the nickname of "Ma Fern." No one knew exactly why but it seemed to fit. Now Ma was a nice person, a truly dedicated teacher and one we were all lucky to have, but we thought she was old, and we really didn't appreciate her as we should have, what with being only fourteen...and nineteen.

One day Bucky decided that it was his duty to call out "Ma Fern," as many times during a forty minute class as he could get away with, just below the level of audible intrusion, a posse of ne'er-do-wells shamelessly counting and marking everything down for posterity.

"Bon jour," our lady addressed the class,

"Ma Fern," our hero would follow, sounding like a small voice from the back corner of the room. We'd start snickering.

"C'est une bon matin," she continued.

"Buc-key," and we were rolling, clutching our desks to our chests, trying not to act involved.

"Ecoutez-moi,"

"*Fern,*" and now we were trying not to piss our pants.

The poor woman paused, gazed over her spectacles at nothing in particular and no doubt at that moment, was probably thinking that she was vastly underpaid.

Bucky was off to the principal's office. Madame Walton, I am *so* sorry. But you see, I couldn't help it, it was so very funny to me.

But that was just the first class of the day. Then we'd move on to English Literature with Mr. Chambers, another trooper from the teaching staff. These teachers had to be on their toes. Tall and distinguished, we would never see him without a yardstick in hand and whenever necessary, with a huge Joker-smile right out of Batman; he would vigorously 'whack' an unsuspecting misbehaver, and there were plenty of those. He did it all in a light-hearted manner but sometimes, even he was pushed to the edge.

Oddly loved and respected by all because of his sense of humor, he was a legend at our school, and a brilliant teacher. The style of his 'whacking' was what set him apart. It would always be in the middle of some Shakespearean phrase and would fall on the downbeat of a sentence,

"Behold, what light through yonder window... *BREAKS*," and the offender would feel the sting of a yardstick on the shoulder. His favorite victim was Bud

Macintosh, another late bloomer in our class. Bud was a rather large and lethargic, brush-cut fellow, whose reputation for not giving a crap must have preceded him because the very first day of school, Mr. Chambers, in dramatic literary voice exclaimed, "*Macintosh*!" and simply pointed his pointer to the preferred spot nearest his desk. With an audible groan, the huge, slow moving lad grudgingly obliged and wedged himself into the front seat. Our fine teacher made the critical mistake however, of seating vice-clown Pete, a mini-me version of the huge Macintosh, right across the aisle. The stage was set.

"With a ho-caw, in a cow's-aah," they would say, a dozen times a day; it was a hidden reference to a certain sexual act between a horse and a cow. I don't know who said it first. I only know that in no time at all, all the guys in class were saying it! We never in our wildest dreams had ever even thought about a thing like this, but it seemed reasonable. Since both these geniuses lived on farms, they obviously knew what the livestock was up to.

Whenever Chambers gave the class an assignment, Big Bud would whisper across the aisle to his trusty sidekick, "Ho-caw!"

Predictable Pete would answer the call, "Cow's-aah!"

Then they'd be off. They would repeat these phrases so often that the challenge would be for them to keep it fresh. Finally one day our esteemed teacher had heard enough and he snapped. He stood in the aisle between them, rearing back and smacking first one and then the other on their thickly padded shoulders, alternating between them while reciting literature... "I have ***slipped*** the surly bonds of earth, and ***danced*** the skies on ***laughter***-silvered ***wings***..."

While this was going on, the two nincompoops took turns, with each blow, loud enough now for the whole class to hear,

"Ho!"...

"Caw!"...

"Cow's!"...

"Aah!"... For me, this made school so worth attending.

Chapter Five

"McArthur's Park is melting in the dark,

All the sweet green icing flowing down..."

-Jim Webb

But the main reason I still loved school was Susan. With her piercing blue eyes and long, silky, light-brown hair, she was to me the sweetest thing walking on God's green earth. I would forever be able to close my eyes and see her in the halls sashaying her perfect body so casually, her model smile brightening my whole day. Usually, the really beautiful girls were so full of themselves they wouldn't give guys like me the time of day. But Susan would always stop and chat.

"Hi, did you understand that math?" she would ask.

"Not I my lady," I would quickly retort, and win a smile. I played the guitar, she had heard about it; that may have had something to do with it, I'll never know.

But senior guys would always be hovering around her and that made me feel helpless. I adored her from a distance for two years! The summer between my junior and senior year was filled with longing. I had no opportunity to see her, unless she happened to be out walking when I'd take Dad's car and make my daily drive down her street to get groceries. When school started again in the fall, her beauty was even more radiant.

The school counselor would probably have said that my extreme infatuation was an escape from the bitter reality at home, but to me, she was so very beautiful! I was madly in love and terrified of finding out that she didn't feel the same way about me, so I kept my feelings hidden and lived in my fantasy. But she must have known. I don't know how she couldn't have.

Many were the blustery nights, while my ailing mother slept in her front bedroom and my exhausted father snored nearby on the couch that I would sit alone in front of the roaring living room fire listening softly to Pet Sounds. In the fire's glow, hot tears rolled down my cheeks, as I thought of the bountiful joy of Susan in my life and the simultaneous frustration over circumstances I just couldn't change.

That year, I let my hair grow very long and began to look like a rock and roller, much to my parent's dismay. It was just the way I was going. This also distanced me from the kind of life that Susan lived. Near the end of our senior year, approaching the time I would have to say goodbye to her, probably forever, a good friend gave me tickets to see Jimi Hendrix at Detroit's Cobo Arena, a once in a lifetime event. I summoned up all of my courage and asked her to go, fully expecting the let down of rejection but unbelievably, she said yes!

Words can't begin to describe the excitement I felt while waiting for that day to arrive. By now she was about as beautiful a woman as I'd ever seen. Like magic, suddenly I was aware that we were holding hands forty rows from center stage. Hendrix entranced us, playing guitar with his teeth while a thousand cameras flashed and all of this only a backdrop for the overwhelming emotion that gripped my heart! After the show we were dropped off at her place and with the gentle good night kiss she gave me on her front porch, as her father flashed the outside light, I grew wings on my heels and floated home just above the sidewalks.

A week later, I nervously asked her out again. I remember it was pouring rain the day she came to my house to say her parents wouldn't let her go. It was the only time she would ever set foot in my place and as we stood on the front porch and she gave me the heartbreaking news, her hair wet, head wistfully cocked to one side, eyes of deepest blue; how lovely you are, was all I could think. What class to face me honestly when the telephone would have been so much easier. Had her parents known how I truly felt about her, they never would have objected, long hair or no.

Late in that summer after graduation, maybe two months later, I got into a rock 'cover' band, imitating the stars while playing the Ontario bar circuit. We worked a tiny club in Stratford, a town known for its Shakespearian festivals. My feelings for Susan never waned but they were only sweet succulent memories that I drew upon dozens of times a day. By a very strange twist of fate, my keyboard player began a relationship with Sue's best friend and through him I was able to keep up with her life.

"Guess what?" the ivory tickler teased me one wonderful day, "Susan is coming here!"

To me, the words rang like a song.

"Susan is coming, Susan is coming!"

She was in college now, and on her own, and there would be no flashing porch light this time. To my last breath, I will never forget Stratford. For one lilac-scented, perfect summer day, she and I walked hand in hand through quaint narrow, brick streets. I felt her skin, listened to her talk, made her laugh, watched her every move, sensing that when she left the next morning, I might never see her again. That night we were so close in the still summer darkness.

Dusk to dawn we lay in a single sleeping bag on the floor, with our clothes on, but even so I gave her all a boy could possibly give to a girl through sweet caress and tender kiss. We never slept. When she left next morning she took a part of me with her and it hurt for a long, long time.

Ten years later, another band I was in did a triumphant, return-home gig right in our little town. I was meeting old friends all night long when suddenly, through a clearing in the crowd; there she sat with her cousin Ray!

It absolutely shocked me. I honestly never thought I'd see her again. She had cute, short hair and her aqua eyes still went right through me. I fell in love all over again.

"Ray told me you were here. It looks like you're doing well," she said. My brain was numb.

"Yeah well, we've had some lucky breaks," I tried to answer. I was thrilled by her energy and enthusiasm. Her eyes were so clear and bright.

"I'm just visiting my Mom and then I'm back to Toronto."

"Toronto, oh great city," I said encouragingly.

But I was thinking, please don't go.

Chapter Six

"We've been friends now for so many years,

We've been together through the fun times

And the tears..."

-The Beach Boys

1964

The summer after that whacky first year of high school, Corey and I buried our toes forever in the clean white sands of Kingsville's beach.

"We've been having fun all summer long," by the Beach Boys would play on our boom box constantly, as we with our raging hormones would make our daily forage for "skin." Of course we would never actually *talk* to any girls; just admire them from a distance.

The changing rooms satisfied our voyeuristic needs. Very basic, they were just enclosed wooden cubicles with a plywood wall between, and it didn't take us long to make the hole. From there, we could get a pretty good eyeful of unsuspecting buns n' boobs! We'd watch for girls, or women, to show signs they were leaving the beach, then hurry and beat them to the changing rooms.

We'd begin to spend so much time at "The Hole," we wouldn't even bother putting on a bathing suit! Wagner was definitely a "tit-man," and that meant the bigger they were, the better he liked them. In fact I couldn't believe how much breast size played a part in his decision-making process! If they had boobs they were babes.

The little bathhouse was basic with a cement floor, no windows, and no electricity. For a gal to change into or out of a bathing suit, meant doing it in the dark. The eyes in the wall would pray for the women's door to open so that the outside light would illuminate the treasures inside. Sometimes Corey would whisper frantically to me,

"Johnny, go and open the ladies' door!" Fearing that I might become the victim of his teasing if I refused, but secretly wanting to see the booty myself, I would oblige, first looking both ways for anyone coming, then I'd reach over and ease my arm against the door, holding it open just enough.

"Who's there?" a concerned voice from within would ask, while heavy breathing would be the only reply. At these moments, I was certain that I was going to hell.

One fine day, my horny pal was at his post when an absolutely gorgeous blonde began to undress, unknowingly, before his frozen eye in the peephole! This was the moment he had been waiting for. As the beads of sweat glistened on his forehead, the men's room door swung open and a stranger entered. My pal couldn't contain his excitement:

"Look at this, look at this!" he whispered. The man peeked into the abyss and pulled back, startled.

"That's my wife, you pervert!" he growled. Corey gasped and made a hasty exit, whimsically saying,

"Sorry!" behind him.

Thinking back to those carefree days, I guess it was then that my rock and roll career must have started. The two of us began talking seriously about playing in public. After school, we would meet at the Wagner's. It was a two-story, white-sided structure with a flower garden filled with lovely tulips and gardenias all around the base of it. Like my own home, the driveway was a car-width lane running along the right side with the side door entrance the most frequently used. I must have come in and out of that door a thousand times.

Mrs. Wagner was a pretty, slender woman with her tinted hair and light pink nails always perfect, effervescence in her voice.

"Hi John, how's your mother?" she would always ask. She was a stay-at-home mom and the atmosphere was warm and cozy. I was always welcomed with a big smile and before anything else was said, offered something to eat. Mr. W. would come home from work with his suit jacket in one hand and the newspaper in the other, give his adoring wife a peck on the cheek and say,

"How was your day honey?"

I felt as though I'd been transported to the set of The Donna Reed Show. The senior Wagner would grab his son and for about a minute, a serious wrestling match would ensue. He reminded me a little of a modern Pa Kettle, short and slender with a prematurely receding hairline, and a matching sense of humor. Sometimes he'd tease me and I wouldn't always get the joke, looking to his sympathetic wife for clues as to how I was to take his gentle ribbing.

"Oh Mac, leave John alone!" she would come to my aid. Lorraine, as wise guy Wagner would call his mom much to my discomfort, would make us sandwiches with potato chips and a pickle. Corey would show his bratty side, complaining about this or that,

"This pickle's *soggy*!" he'd whine, but I'd always say,

"Thank you Mrs. Wagner, everything is delicious as always." I knew this kind of butt kissing was the way to get invited back but it also *was* delicious. We'd wolf everything down in the TV room and then hurry to the front room to practice our songs.

My buddy would thump away on his plastic snare drum from the Eaton's catalogue, and to keep his mom happy he'd muffle it with a tea towel. Both of us would sing our heads off and it was pure joy! I loved that my buddy could sing high like Brian Wilson. My own fingers would be raw from strumming madly on a flimsy acoustic guitar, but even so, I hated to stop. We'd only break to watch Robin Seymour's 'Swingin' Time,' or Dick Clark's American Bandstand, see what The Beatles or Beach Boys were doing, and then with renewed inspiration, go right back at it. In a little while, dinner would be ready and if I didn't get the usual invitation from the gracious Mrs. Wagner, it was my cue to go.

It was a nice time in my life, living in Kingsville, and although I would feel guilty about not spending more time with my ailing mother, I couldn't help being a teenager. She had gotten steadily worse and now could not speak above a whisper. This meant that if she and I were going to communicate, I would have to slow down, get quiet, and listen. In the evenings I could do that but during the day it was almost impossible. I would stream through the house on my way to something I perceived as musically significant, lost in my own little world.

"Goin' to Corey's, back for supper," I'd say, the screen door already closing behind me. I sang and hummed and bounced around in those days, despite my mother's quiet suffering. But best of all, I had music in my life.

Chapter Seven

"Say where did we go?

Days when the rains came

Down in a hollow

Playin' a new game..."

-Van Morrison

1965

We called our first band the Y-Knotts. Corey beat his drum, tea towel removed, while Billy, a kid whose instrument was almost as tall as he was, and I played our Sears-catalogue electric guitars. Both the bass and lead were plugged into the same 25-watt amplifier, played at volume "10," and the sound was pure distortion, like a swarm of overweight bees! Nevertheless, it was really exciting for me to have bass in our sound.

Billy was the kind of kid that Wagner probably ordinarily would never have hung around with. He wasn't cool in the typical sense. He was on the shorter side with kind of a round figure. But he was a good sort and always cheerful. His passion was racing motorcycles and their house was overflowing with his trophies. No, they weren't each other's type but the common desire to *rock and roll* wiped all that out. It was a miracle, really, and

I'd see it again and again over the years. Music seemed to erase all boundaries.

As we fifteen-year-olds practiced loudly, Billy's mom, who I thought looked exactly like Mrs. Claus, would rock back and forth, tapping her knees, in complete delight.

"You boys sound *wonderful*!" the jolly lady would gush gleefully after each song, and we started to believe it too. When Billy's sister got married, we were hired to play at the reception, in between the Polka Band's sets. We made twenty-five bucks and thought we were rich! Eventually, Billy started to travel, racing his bikes all over Canada, and that effectively ended the Y-Knotts.

Then came The Small Town Boys. There would only be a dozen people who would remember them, and half of those would be the band members themselves. But it came about at the perfect time for me. Boy did it ever. The Beatles were in full bloom, with the Rolling Stones closing in. A host of groups like The Lovin' Spoonful, The Turtles, and Spanky and Our Gang rattled the airwaves with great little pop gems that everybody loved. Summers were peaceful and easy as Corey and I forged our friendship, practicing our rock and roll songs in his living room at every possible opportunity.

One day, he greeted me at his door with some exciting news:

"Johnny, I know these two guys from the States, and they're really cool... and they wanna' start a band!"

It was as though a rocket had launched up my spine! Play in a real band with American guys? Are you kidding? This is what I wanted to do more than anything in the world! All Americans knew how to rock n roll!

"And guess what?" he continued to astound me,

"They live on Cedar Island!" At 16, it seemed as though every 24 hours, there was a new door to open, another gift to unwrap, but this topped everything! By the time Saturday rolled around, and I had been given a few more details, the new guys had achieved mythical status.

It was a blue-sky day and my buddy managed to get, as he called it, the "Pig-mobile," the family's huge white 1964 Ford Galaxy. To this day I'm not sure why he called it that but it seemed to go along with the times. With windows wide, we practically flew the two miles down the two-lane lake road to the island. The kind of excitement and anticipation we felt then, cruising to our destiny, warm breezes mixed with cologne, swirling inside the car, radio blasting, land yacht swaying gently over worn shocks, Corey tapping out the beat with one cracked drumstick on the dashboard; life for me would never be quite that sweet again.

I'm sure I looked like a happy deer in the headlights.

We rendezvoused at Brent Wall's house a couple of blocks from the beach and our new cohorts were sitting on the front porch when we pulled in, their feet swinging nervously. Brent was a clean-cut, stocky, shorthaired kid with a "don't mess with me" expression on his face. Kind of a tough guy, when I showed him the bass line to "Ain't Seen Nothin' Yet" by the Blues Magoos, he melted like butter and I finally saw him smile! But he did a good job of hiding that smile.

"So this is the rock star, huh Wag'?" he said, signaling the 'all-clear' to me. He had a beautiful Hofner bass that looked exactly like Paul McCartney's. I couldn't take my eyes off of it! To me, this was all *unbelievable.* Inside, I was still a Mennonite farm boy.

The other Yank was Lonnie Mack, a thin, Buddy Holly-ish kid, about 5-5, who wore his hair in a 'greaser' style and seemed to always have one hand in his front blue jean pocket and a lit cigarette in the other. I didn't have to show him *anything.* He was 'bad!' In our world, guys were either frats or greasers and it was the first time I had met someone that walked the line in between, and didn't care.

Lonnie wasn't good looking in the usual sense but he had a tremendous cool reserve. Not lost on me was the fact that, then and during our coming years together, never would less than two gorgeous girls be chasing him at any one time! It gave an ordinary looking guy like me, a lot of hope! He wore thick, dark-rimmed glasses, and had 'street' savvy, and the streets he was savvy to were Detroit's! He could sing and play the guitar extremely well, but his specialty was the Hammond B3 organ. *Man* could he *wail* on that thing!

He was the most talented person I had ever known and at 17, the senior member of our new group! I loved how Lonnie would put on a most serious 'bad-ass' face one second, and then crack up completely, eyes enlarged through thick, coke-bottle lenses, the next! He had a great sense of humor. He liked to call each of us "faggot," to unnerve us and then he'd win us over by cracking his award-winning smile.

"Hey faggot, when we gonna' start rehearsing?" he would ask me at the end of our first day together, then gave me my first, Black man's handshake, while chuckling at himself. These were white guys with soul! I liked them both right away and had no problem committing to being in a band with them.

As far as my folks were concerned, I figured sooner or later I'd have to tell them I was playing rock and roll but I didn't feel the need to say anything right now; only that I'd found some American friends.

"You should...hang around...with your own...kind," my mother whispered after I eventually told her the news.

"And do what?" I dared to speak out,

"Drive around Leamington in a pickup truck?" I thought I was in for it but this time for some reason, my Pop didn't say anything.

The Small Town Boys began practicing every day we all could at the Mack cottage on the beach, setting up on their wide summer lakeside porch, around the huge organ. It was difficult because all of us worked a summer job. Brent and Corey cut lawns and I worked on Mr. Kraus' farm several days a week, cutting asparagus, picking beans, and driving tractor. Lonnie was poised to take over his father's moving business and worked so many hours, driving 50 miles to the States every day with his Dad, it was a wonder he even had time to be in a band!

At his invitation, I tagged along with him one blistering August day in 1966, a year before the riots, on the gritty streets of Detroit. I'll never forget it. Our job was simple. Go into a neighborhood in the heart of the city, and move furniture, including a piano, out of a burn-damaged *third* floor apartment, down three flights of stairs, with a turn at each floor, and out into our step van. I hadn't seen Detroit since I was a 4-year-old kid, when Mom had taken Frances and me by bus to the downtown Hudson store to meet Santa.

This was very different.

As we went about the task, members of the household began accusing one another of setting the fire that had caused all the damage. A very serious argument ensued, much to my dismay, and pretty soon, folks were in the street in various stages of undress, and complete chaos, while Lonnie and I covertly kept doing our job! The police were summoned but long before they arrived, a sister-in-law inside the house suddenly produced a shiny meat cleaver and attacked her brother-in-law!

" You tried 'ta burn my house down, moth-a-*fuck*-ah, Ah'll *kiy'* 'yo *moth*-a-fuck-in' ass*! "*

Shocked by the language alone, my eyeballs grew large as I saw the terror, in the near-victim's face. He flew down the narrow steps, just past me, she shortly behind, slashing left and slashing right, blade shining even in the dimly lit stairwell, barely missing him on each swipe! There was no doubt she would have killed him had she caught up with him. "Aw just act like you don't notice," Lonnie would say matter-of-factly! Mack was one of the coolest people under fire, I would ever know. Fortunately, the knife never found its mark and we would finish our job under the watchful eyes of the Detroit Police's "Big Four," who finally arrived to calm things down. But I was still shaking like a leaf as we drove away.

"That's nothin'" my partner sighed, his elbow out the window, lit cigarette in the steering hand,

"I'll take you someplace, show 'ya somethin' fa' real."

"No thanks, I've seen enough." I gulped.

It was my good friend Lonnie who showed me the beauty and value in soul music. Up to that point it had been all pop and rock for me. When, from his sisters' vast rhythm and blues album collection, a Motown or

'Philly' tune would play on the family's gigantic stereo, he would close his eyes and with lit cigarette, he would begin dancing, not a lot of arm flailing and gyrating, but smooth and casual, the way the black guys did.

Both hands would be curled in front of his chest and he'd clench and relax, just slightly, to the fat backbeat. The Pall Mall smoke would weave its own dance while his eyes, magnified through thick lenses, would stare straight out. His feet knew all the steps.

Chapter Eight

"I'm a Soul man,

I'm a Soul man..."

-Sam and Dave

1967

In a Mennonite home, dancing and rock music were considered evil and strictly forbidden, even though I always saw plenty of Mennonite kids at all the hops. Hanging with Lonnie, for me, all of that thinking went out the window. Sometimes, there would be a dozen kids doing steps in the Mack living room to their loud, funky stereo! Line dancing spontaneously in somebody's living room; this was so cool! It was "dirty" dancing, way before Dirty Dancing!

We'd bring that same feeling to our rehearsals. Before the Small Town Boys would practice, Mack would fire up that big B3 organ. The bell speakers inside the two gigantic Leslie oil cabinets would begin to spin, slowly at first, then faster and faster, according to the Master's command and when we played Sam and Dave's "Soul Man," even the grown ups within earshot could not help but have goose bumps!

I did some things I wasn't so proud of in those days; things my mother was probably afraid I would do. Tommy and Eddie, cousins about a year younger whose folks also had cottages nearby, became our constant companions and biggest fans, cheering us on, picking songs to learn, and acting as 'roadies'.

Tommy's grandfather, "Pops," had a cottage just down the lane from Lonnie's and one hot August night, Pops was magically visiting friends out of town. This was no less than a call to arms for our 'posse.' The cute little bungalow, with a fabulous picture window full of Lake Erie, was quaint and cozy but of principal interest to us was the well-stocked liquor cabinet! We could easily have our fill and Tommy would replace the missing amounts with water! This would be my first taste of 'hard stuff' and from that day on and forever more, the smell of lemon gin would conjure up for me, wildly spinning memories.

"I love you guys," I gushed as I lay in front of the cottage on the damp grass, wondering why I had drank so much and also wondering if I had anything left in me to throw up.

"Thpew, thpew, never again," I spat. The boys babysat, God-Bless-um, placing cold wet facecloths on my head. I really did love them. For a little old Mennonite boy, I felt lucky to be included in this group. Because of my ability to make music, which was such a wonderful gift that had been given to me, I was allowed into the inner sanctum of cool.

Corey, Lonnie, Brent, Eddie, and Tommy all taught me about fashion, good music, and what girls liked. In the teenage guy-world, this was everything. In turn, whatever I lacked in 'cool,' I think I made up for with musical leadership. The Small Town Boys sang four-part harmonies in tune, and played rock and roll! What a band we were! And we were the best of friends too so it was nothing but fun. We practiced more than we actually performed but we didn't care. It was all about making a joyful noise. And we certainly did that.

It was our goal to be good enough to be asked to play at Surfside 3. A covered roller rink with a huge, cement dance floor and open sides, the "Surf" drew excited kids from as far away as Michigan and Ohio to see national pop acts perform live, and to dance, on Friday and Saturday nights. The quality of acts that came through there, and the constant radio ads on the big Windsor station, C K R W, had put Kingsville on the map, so far as we young folks were concerned. All the Motown stars came through Surfside; The Temptations, The Miracles, The Supremes. Bob Seger cut his teeth there with his band, The Lost Herd. Dick Clark even brought the magnetic Paul Revere and The Raiders!

On any given night, at least half the crowd was from the States and half of those would be hot looking chicks! It was the only place to be! Fridays would come and after hanging out in excited anticipation at the beach all day, Corey and I would go our separate ways by five o'clock in the afternoon and through a series of coded phone calls, find out who could get "wheels." I would primp in front of the mirror for a few minutes; tell my folks I was going to the beach, and after their ever-weakening protests, run the 8 minutes over to Wagner's house.

Lorraine would shout from somewhere inside as soon as she heard my clicking heels on the driveway,

"Just go right on upstairs, John!" and halfway up, the overpowering smell of English Leather would make me weak in the knees. He wore so much cologne that I didn't need to wear any! Surfer Girl would be playing on the small portable turntable, as both of us would drool over a Playboy, priming us for things hoped for.

"I hope that blonde chick is there tonight," Corey would say in a cocky, course whisper, smacking his gum.

"I'm gonna' deal 'er---oh look at this," as he'd turn the big double page sideways. I'd try not to stare too long.

He always wore the coolest clothes, and though his shiny, wavy blonde hair was perfect to begin with, he'd still spend half an hour getting it just right. Finally he'd be ready, pour even more cologne on his shirt, give his mom a peck on the cheek, and we'd *Pig-mobile* to Linden Beach, where the rest of the crew would be waiting patiently. Soon, the magnificent six would be on their way, Eddie and Tommy, Ben and Lonnie, and Corey and me.

We'd make the scene at Surfside and life was good. I will never forget the soft, warm summer breezes that flowed around us, the hundreds of smells, excited voices, girls in tight jeans, and the crashing sounds of live bands in the open air. And the ridiculous way the guys would *all* go 'round one way, while the girls would *all* go 'round the other.

During those days, I told my parents only what they needed to know and anything more than that, they wouldn't have understood anyway. They came from and were living in, another world. I lied a few times too back then, but had I not done so, I would have missed the companionship of some really great guys and the opportunity to be in The Small Town Boys.

The Vietnam War brought us all out of the dream. Lonnie got the dreaded letter from his draft board. It was a rainy fall day when I helped him cover up his B3 and we said goodbye.

"I'll be back in two years and we'll go from there," he reassured, staring quietly out over the lake from behind the coke bottle glasses. But I wondered. As the dying golden maple leaves left the safety of their arbors and fluttered to the cold ground, I remember thinking that with Lonnie, the army had sure picked a good man. Like so many young Americans of that time, Tommy and Eddie sat on pins and needles too, until their letters came and told them they could stay home for now.

Sadly, around this time Wagner lost interest in playing music and gave up the drums. I thought it was a crying shame and tried to talk him out of it, but to no avail. As talented as Corey was, he would certainly have been one of the best around. I was as shocked as I could be. Everything seemed to change over night.

That year, Eddie and Tommy moved back to the States and I never saw nor heard from them again. As far as the other guys, I would run into each of them, only a couple of times over the many years, on rare visits back to Kingsville. I was always sorry for not keeping in closer contact with the friends that had meant so much to me, but life just took us all in other directions and certainly, to far away places.

I often thought, over the years, how neat it would be to get the whole gang; some that had become grandfathers, back together again, before it was too late. The magnificent six would walk once more, down the remote winding road that circled the island, near the end of a hot, sultry Cedar Island summer day. We'd talk about 'skin' as a Rascals tape would play, with constant Lake Erie to our left the way it used to be, when life was simple and wonderful.

Chapter Nine

"Somethin' happenin' here,

What it is, ain't exactly clear,

There's a man with a gun over there,

Telling me, I got to beware..."

-Buffalo Springfield.

1968

Most of my Canadian friends were oblivious to the Vietnam War, except as the grizzly images on NBC's Huntley-Brinkley Report would remind them. I felt it, because my association with Lonnie's folks didn't stop just because he wasn't around. They continued to welcome me in their home as one of their own and spoke openly and frankly in my presence, as did the folks of my other Yank friends. That's what I loved about them, their total acceptance of and hospitality toward me. They'd carry on as though I were one of their own sons,

"Goddangit Biff, you cain't be workin' all those hours, I cain't run this place by myself!" Lonnie's mom would say.

"Aw shushup! Who's gonna' pay the bills then?" would be the frustrated reply.

They would argue a little, then make up and dance around the living room to the stereo that was always playing Johnny Cash or Patsy Cline!

"Oh you get me so hoppin' mad," she'd sway, smacking him on the shoulder, fighting the tiny smile that threatened her face. They loved each other deeply. Jenny Mack's eyes always looked tired. As a young girl, she had watched her husband go off to Korea and now, there was her firstborn son, in Vietnam. She would read parts of Lonnie's letters aloud:

"Tell the fellahs, I'm a killing machine now so they better not give me any lip when I get back!"

The lover of all things good was anything but that. He had been stationed near the fighting and would probably have gone into the thick of it, had fate not intervened. One day near the Officer's Mess, feeling homesick and alone, he had sat at an old upright piano and began playing the blues and some soulful gospel tunes. He could play like Liberace when he wanted to. A small crowd had gathered.

"Ten-Hut!" a voice boomed, signaling an officer present, as the enlisted men stood stock-straight.

"Don't stop playing son," was the order from the Colonel of the base, and Lonnie continued. This time, he broke into 'Amazing Grace,' and before he was through, there were tears in all eyes, including the Colonel's. Lonnie was given the job of chauffer for the last few months of his hitch so he would always be on hand to play his beautiful music in the mess! Unlike many young sons, some that had become his friends, Lonnie came home intact, mercifully saved from the front lines.

The day he set foot back on Cedar Island and the Mack's threw a big welcome home party, Lonnie, still with lit cigarette between fingers, uncharacteristically hugged all of us tightly, calling each of us, "asshole," or "dickhead." Never before had the terms been so endearing.

During this time I had been working part time at old Mr. Krause's farm, picking beans and cutting asparagus. It was hot work and I complained, but I did it. By the end of the day, somehow I would finish whatever old Mr. K had given me to do. The pay was minimal, about a dollar a basket but if I worked enough hours, I made out all right. I was happy. My goal was to someday get a white Fender Stratocaster like the one Jimi Hendrix had and I fully believed I was going to make it.

At some point I let Eddie Malloy, a close and very persuasive friend; talk me into enrolling at Tangent's Turkey Farm. The Malloy's owned the Marina on Cedar Island. Ed was a wiry little tough guy who always kept his head cocked to one side. I don't know why but sometimes when I walked down the street with him, I found myself cocking my own head to one side. There we would be; two guys with their heads to one side for no apparent reason.

No wonder he could talk me into such a horrible job like inseminating turkeys!

It was our task to *de*-seminate the 'toms' by sucking on a long glass tube, and *in*-seminate the hens by reversing the process. Often just spreading the turkey's legs would cause a geyser of shit to soar into the air, spraying everyone in range! Starting at midnight, it promised 2 dollars an hour, a whopping amount for teenage labor at that time! There was a damn good reason.

By morning's light, we'd be covered with turkey crap from head to toe! I remember being grateful for working at night when it was at least a little cooler and smelled a little less awful! Eddie's cousin Dick was our foreman and since he was only 2 years older than the rest of us, we goofed around a lot. Sometimes, if it was too hot, we didn't work at all. We would all try to gang tackle "Big," only one of the many nicknames we had for him, finally hauling him down in a heap, in the shit-strewn corral!

At the end of our shift, just as the golden sun peeked over the trees, and the temperature began to rise in the hot Ontario mid-summer, we'd take off our coveralls and throw them in Dick's trunk for the long ride home. Believe you me; it was gamey in *that* car!

As we pulled up in front of my house one morning, before getting out, I asked our cheerful foreman why we had to do a job like that and without missing a beat he casually answered,

"Because turkeys are too dumb to fuck!"

The sound of us guys hee-hawing in the car probably woke the whole neighborhood! This was the kind of humor that I had begun to love, as I would unlock the side door and quietly let myself back into my sedate Mennonite home.

Being seniors in high school, crazy Malloy and I were thick as thieves for a time. We'd both skip some classes, meet downtown, and shoot pool. Except for seeing Susan, school had lost all appeal for me. In fact, for me, life in that area was so boring that if there had been any way, I would gladly have left town!

One month before final exams, cocked-headed Eddie came to me with a serious proposal. It involved "Mr. T.," the man who owned the turkey farm.

"He wants us to be foremen at his Mexico plant!"

Wow, I thought! A foreman in Mexico!

There was even talk of "women servants!"

As a consequence of this, bow-fuss idiots blew off our final exams. This was despite the fact that we had gone to school the whole year, with better than average grades! One week after summer vacation started, and as report cards were being mailed, Malloy called me with the news:

"Uh, change of plans, Mr. T. wants us to stay in school and get a good education!"

I had crapped in my pants only once before, high jumping with diarrhea, but this would be a close second! How would I ever explain this to my folks? After a long unscheduled meeting, the school board agreed to give two boneheaded turkey farmers a break, and we each received our diploma.

Chapter Ten

"When you're down, and troubled,
And you need a helping hand..."

-Carol King.

1973

I couldn't stand the idea of more schooling. All I wanted to do was play music. Over the next 5 years, I was a working musician, playing in un-illustrious bar bands all over Michigan, Ohio and Ontario, keeping up with the bills and developing my stage chops. My drummer friend Richie Vane had bounced from band to band with me and we had become close as brothers. We shared the same philosophy and had similar musical tastes and dreams. At that time I wanted to be Jimi Hendrix and Richie played the drums in a style close to Mitch Mitchell, Hendrix's drummer.

His long curly hair would fly as he bobbed and weaved while expressing his percussive talents behind his drum set. He made faces when he played, squeezing out every last ounce of rhythmic delights and people loved to watch him. His Hollywood smile and dynamic drum solos would bring down the house. We played loud and hard every night and loved every minute of it but after that many years of spinning our wheels, we needed a break. Richie went to a commune in Colorado to find himself while I went home to be with my folks.

It was during this time that my mother passed away. She had suffered much for many years and in some ways, her death was a relief. Eventually I would cry. I wanted to include the story of her life between these pages but it was just too sad. Anyone who has watched a loved one suffer knows whereof I speak.

I stayed in Kingsville for a while after that living at my Dad's and keeping him company while playing in local bands. It was a great relationship I now had with the old boy. I rocked and rolled at night in this small rural area where I had grown up and visited with him during the day. Every once in a while he could really make me laugh. One night as we sat at the kitchen table, he gave me his time-tested remedy for hemorrhoids.

"Raw turnips, they'll put tips on your turds like that," he said with a wicked grin, his thumb and forefinger an inch apart. He was an easy person to be around, but creatively I was at an all-time low point in my life. I had no career, and no prospects. I never stopped writing songs but they remained unrecorded and unheard by anyone.

Richie came back from Colorado just in time. He was renewed and refreshed, a bounce in every step of his tight muscular frame, his blue eyes shining with fire.

"Faye McGill told me that if we want to come to Vegas, she'll put us up," he enthused over breakfast at Pop's one morning. My dad listened quietly, crunching his Shredded Wheat. I had heard the Faye McGill story a few times. She was a large, affable, lady who played the piano and told jokes. Discovered by Liberace, she now was the main headliner of the Sands Hotel on the strip in Vegas and would be there for a whole year.

She and my friend must have been on similar spiritual paths because they wound up at the same commune in Colorado and in only a short time, despite her being much older, had become good friends. Any other time I wouldn't have given a crap about Vegas, all those milk-toasted white-suited assholes and their flaccid music, but I was desperate. So it was that on a snowy March morning, in a newly painted, competition orange, 6-year-old Cadillac Hurst, after a solemn goodbye to my dad and Richie's mom, we hit the road! Each of us had everything he owned in the back of the customized funeral coach and about five hundred dollars in his pocket. I hoped and prayed something would happen before my money ran out because I did *not* want to have to come back and work in those dives again.

In the evening of the third day, we broke through a clearing in the mountains and there before us in the distance, glowing like some Arabian secret in the middle of the dry Nevada desert, was Las Vegas! Cruising slowly down the strip, in our beautifully restored, bright orange limousine, we were suddenly a part of the show, a festival of lights and signs, voluptuous women and handsome men dressed to the 'nines,' and beautiful, vintage automobiles. I couldn't believe the glitz and glamour. It was overwhelming. I was the happiest that moment that I had been in a long time.

"Come in, come in," Faye beckoned with outstretched arm, and with that, we entered a brand new world, the likes of which I had never seen.

"I'll let cha stay for three weeks, How's that?" The large blonde woman in blue eye shadow, wearing a dashika offered as she walked before us, giving two wide-eyed musicians a guided tour of her luxurious home. I had never seen a garage door opener, or a dishwasher! We each had our own room and since Faye was practically never there, the whole house too! When she *was* there, she was always on the phone talking to agents, managers or producers. One day she carried on with someone named Lee and after she hung up chortled,

"He is such a cut-up."

"Who's that?" I asked nosily.

"Oh, Lee...you know, Liberace!"

I had literally gone from being completely down and out as a musician, to being one degree away from rubbing elbows with the biggest stars in the world, in about a week! In her den was a bulletin board covered with Polaroid's of her and all the big stars including the entire Rat Pack. I wrote my pop and told him all about it, but a few months later heard him ask,

"What's a Rat Pack?"

Through Faye's connections we found work in a traveling band that passed through Vegas, but was headed for parts unknown. Now I had to wear short hair and the tacky clothes I had once so despised. I was now the, "milk-toasted white-suited asshole!" We were living out of our suitcases, bouncing from town to town, one week here, two there, but at least we were working. The goal was to tighten up the show and bring it back to the glitzy city.

Mike was our keyboard player and to say he was entertaining was a vast understatement. He was from New Jersey and he came by his sense of humor honestly. He was the great-nephew of Lou Costello. Shiny black curls and deep blue eyes, he was the star of our show and the ladies couldn't take their eyes off of him. A marvelous dancer, singer, and mime, as good as he was on stage, the after-gig parties were never dull. I became very close with him and together we fashioned some wild comedy bits, some of which were too risqué for our audiences. But we sure laughed when Mike turned the sound off on the TV and did his own dialogue.

Days for us would be filled with going to Laundromats, finding the nearest music store, practicing, or eating in restaurants. Nights it was all about putting on the best show we could. After, we'd gather in one of our motel rooms, sometimes with the ladies from the wait staff, and party until the sun came up. We consumed truckloads of beer and smoked lots of weed. Some gigs were okay; some were less so.

In sleepy Salina, Kansas one night, I was in the middle of my fiddle routine when unexpectedly, a huge, bearded 'good ole boy' jumped up on the stage, wrapped his arms around me from behind and lifted me so high into the air, that I was upside down! I had never played the fiddle upside down. I guess in his own dumb ass way, he was paying me a compliment. The bouncers just stood there laughing. The only way out was to pretend to enjoy it, just keep smiling even when it hurt. The boys behind me broke into circus music.

"Ladies and gentlemen, how about a big hand for Billy Bob the Magnificent and our own John David," Mike ad-libbed laughing hysterically as I glared at him, upside down. The crowd ate it up.

And for me, pleasing the audience was always the bottom line.

Chapter Eleven

"When a problem comes along, you must whip it..."

-Devo.

1978

Life on the road was no fun after a while, as any salesman knows. No home base, constantly eating in restaurants of whose history we had no knowledge, no lasting relationships. It was a life-full of strangers. In the beginning it was exciting but after three years, it *sucked.* Richie and I wanted to get back to our roots of playing rock and roll so we went back to Southern Ontario. Although in our youthful arrogance we thought of that area as a cultural wasteland it felt *good* to see our families again.

Going back to blue jeans, we put a gritty little rock band together and kicked ass six nights a week in Windsor at a place called The Ottawa Tavern. That felt good too. It was the usual raunchy beer bar and all that goes with it, but it was much more. We soon began to feel like part of a joyously dysfunctional family! Men's and Ladies baseball teams would celebrate their wins or losses over too many pitchers of draft beer and inevitably, while everyone danced and grooved to our music, someone's pants would fly across the room.

And the guys were just as bad.

Sometimes, and in the band's view quite delightfully so, the whole boat seemed ready to tip over! I would pick up the fiddle once or twice every night as a special feature and we would play a country number that went nervously fast at the end, a holdover from our show band days. Each time we did it, a huge ironworker named Mo would drunkenly waddle from the draft room to the band's side of the tavern, giving a raucous, four-hundred-and-fifty pound rebel yell as he came! There was no stopping him. To attempt to do so would have been suicidal. The giant man could have *shouted* someone to death!

Only I would be on the dance floor, fiddling away with the boy's behind me on the small, elevated stage. I'd gingerly step aside with what I was told was a wicked smile, to let Mo do his 'act!' As the frantic music grew in intensity, the fire in the gargantuan man's eyes would ignite the screaming patrons...they knew what was next! He would turn his huge rear end to the crowd, give his band a last look and, "*AAAAUUGH*," he would scream with squinted eyes, in a voice that bellowed above our roaring amplifiers. As his gigantic trousers dropped to the floor Richie's cymbals crashed perfectly!

This would give the, by now startled audience, a picture in their minds that would be impossible to forget! Two road-map wrinkled, humungous, sofa-pillow size butt cheeks sandwiching the largest set of human clappers anyone had ever seen, or would ever see, made it a night to remember for even the most casual observer! From the back, it was impossible to tell if it was a human, or an elephant!

"Ahhhh...no fiddle tonight, okay fellas?" our beleaguered boss would be waiting to say solemnly in his deepest voice, when we would arrive at the club, signaling Mo's presence in the draught room.

Poor man.

He was trying to run a clean establishment, but with regulars like Mo, it was darned near impossible. On one hand, I would be relieved, but on the other, the fat man was pretty damn entertaining! Especially for our pal Richie, who absolutely loved it! He would laugh so hard, tears would be streaming down his face as he tried to keep the beat on his drums, and this was a *very* professional musician. Soon neither band nor crowd could keep composure, realizing the sheer absurdity of it all! Richie's laugh is what made it so funny to me. If we couldn't make it big, at least laughing at life made things bearable.

Now in my late twenties, I was restless for a meaningful relationship with a loving woman. I couldn't seem to find a keeper in these places I performed, at least not one that I could fall in love with, until I met Grace. She had come into the club with a girlfriend and I was smitten from the first look. Like Cher she had long straight hair that hung full and shiny all the way down past her butt. The biggest, most loving brown eyes melted me in my shoes and I simply had to get to know her.

By the time a few months had gone by we had become very close. She was American and lived in Michigan with her two young boys Michael and Jason. Although I sensed that I was biting off a mouthful, I really loved Grace. During my many visits to her place over the coming year I got to know and love the boys also and soon I couldn't picture my life without them. We were married in her home by the mayor of Romulus with all of our closest friends and family in attendance. It was a beautiful service. My Dad was there and so was Richie's mom Sal, who had been like a mother to me. Richie stood as my best man. I was very content.

Soon our daughter Julia came along and the moment I held her in my arms I knew my life had changed forever. She was adorable and so very lovely. Her brothers loved her too and her arrival cemented our family the way nothing else could have. I was booked for the next eighteen years!

Chapter Twelve

"Hey look around, leaves are brown now,

And the sky is a hazy shade of winter..."

-Paul Simon

1985

Despite the happy home lives we now enjoyed Richie and I took turns dealing with the frustration of still being invisible to the music business while no prospects of any change loomed over the horizon. When we were a little younger, things seemed to happen fast without much effort, but now, approaching our thirties, our careers moved in slow motion. We had tried everything that was possible for us to try, for 13 years. We had recorded, sent out songs, and been rejected hundreds of times. Artistically, our tanks were empty.

One cool fall morning, we hugged for the last time like the brothers we had become. With his pretty new wife Pam, he was going to make a life in California, and this time there'd be no coming back. I watched their taillights disappear, then went down to my quiet little basement studio, locked the door, and felt a loneliness bordering on despair. It was like experiencing two deaths, one being my best friend and the other, the mysterious 'something' that visited whenever we had made music together. As I sobbed aloud in the darkened room, my head rested wearily on my arms and 13 years of tears poured down to the carpet below.

From the time my mother had died in 1975, Dad had continued on by himself in the lovely old, two-story red brick house on Queen Street in Kingsville. I felt bad that he was alone when I was on the road, but he seemed to like his life there, befriending all the children in the neighborhood, offering them his open front porch as a sanctuary from whatever was going on up and down the street. The kids called him "Mister." He had also become interested in local politics, showing up at every town meeting in his green carpenter work clothes, standing to voice his disapproval at some of the brain trust's more inane policies.

"Good grief, we can't allow tractor trailers to park on our streets. It's dangerous for the little ones!" he would stand and deliver.

As I was growing up, he had always been the archetypal Mennonite father, strong and silent, but hidden from all but his closest was an active and unusual sense of humor. He would make some very odd, low and high-pitched sounds around the house, like a human conure.

"Oh-Boy!" some character's musical voice would come out of him. He never watched cartoons in his life to my knowledge, but you'd never know it. He had better voices than *anybody*. I recognized from an early age that those sounds meant that it was a good time to ask him for stuff. While my poor dad would be looking forward to a nice Sunday afternoon snooze, Frances and I would start tugging at him and beg to be taken to Marentette Beach. He'd respond with a "hee-haw" sound and wouldn't move until finally, after he'd been pestered long enough he'd take us and there, under a shade tree; would continue his nap!

I was glad that, through all the years, my father and I never had a falling out. As time flew by, the big, gentle man had become more and more precious to me and I grew to love him as a great old friend. More than that, I was in awe of him. Frank had always tried to make it at least once to our local gigs. Even during his 60s he didn't seem to age, and I had only noticed slightly more graying with each visit. I was glad when he began building his beautiful furniture out of his home, and no longer had to crawl under houses on hands and knees, or cling precariously to their roofs, as he had done for over 35 years.

But I still worried about him being alone.

I was married now and living in Michigan, and as I would commute each day to Windsor to play the bars, I watched an amazing thing begin to happen. Richie, still a year away from making his big move to California, began to hang out with my Pop. He would drive thirty miles each day from Windsor to be with him, and to hang out. Even when we had been younger, my spirited friend had always talked to my father, unlike some of my other friends that avoided parental confrontations. Sometimes, as teenagers, I would have to take my dear friend by the elbow and steer him out of the house or he and my father would have kept talking all day! His own father's sudden passing when he was only nine, had robbed him of a mature father-son relationship.

Now, he was calling my dad, "Papa," and spent his days at 108 Queen, drilling, nailing, painting, sawing, and anything else the old man needed help with. At night when we would meet at the Ottawa to play, my pal would recount with glee, stories of what he and my father had accomplished that day. It was wonderful. It was a great comfort to me, knowing my father was being watched over in this way. After Richie moved to California, their relationship continued over the telephone and through the mail.

Papa turned 71 and a few weeks after that, called me to ask if I could take him for some tests that had been scheduled in a Windsor hospital. I began to feel uneasy. The diagnosis was not promising. The doctor somberly placed his hands on my father's big shoulders and said,

"Well Frank, should things not go according to plan, you've had 71 good years."

The operation, which was risky at best, was to take place as soon as possible in a London hospital, two hours away. A few days later, as the two of us drove silently on the 401, the rolling dairy farms of Southern Ontario drifting by my window, the lazy cows in the beautiful sunshine belying the gravity of the moment, I felt as though I had slipped into a dreamscape. Dad spoke quietly of things he had never mentioned before, where all his papers were and the will and other things I might need to know but I pooh-poohed all of it!

"Dad, you're gonna be fine, you're as strong as an ox!" I would encourage.

"Well Johnson," he replied in a light-hearted chuckle, "Maybe not this time," and the silence that followed was deafening.

Frances was living in British Columbia at the time and the wise old man insisted she be called which only added to my concern. She arrived out of breath the night before the big event and her little brother was never so glad to see his big sister again! Once again she had my back. We sat quietly with him, Frances on one side and I on the other, holding his big, rough, gentle hands until late into the night. He spoke softly about his life and our mother. He was still in love with her, ten years after her death.

He seemed to know he was near the end because he mentioned everything that would need to be handled and we realized he had all his ducks in a row. He talked about Richie and the terrific year they had spent together, building things, fixing things. I could see in my father's face that it had been true quality time for him. That night I called my best friend in California and shocked him with the news. He had started teaching percussion during the day and was gigging at night in Hollywood, making successive strides but with a recession in full swing.

Times were very tough for him, but without hesitation he said, "I'm coming up!"

I assured him that everything was going to be all right and that for now he should just sit tight. But it was only false bravado. After a sleepless night, early the next morning Frances and I walked slowly alongside our father's gurney and held his hands once again, a little tighter this time. We went as far as the rules would allow and then each leaned and hugged our dear dad and said,

"I love you, see you in a little while," and the man of a few words said the same to us and squeezed each of our hands tightly. As the attendants wheeled him slowly around the corner, he gave one last wink, a thumbs-up, and was gone.

The man who had shown his children more by his actions than his words; this wonderful husband who had stood so unwaveringly by his wife's side for so long; this kind and always patient man who had let his son's loud rock band set up in his living room and practice late into the night when he had needed his sleep; this simple, gentle, giant of a man with the compassionate spirit, who had welcomed the little neighborhood kids to play on his porch in protection and safety every day...was gone.

Richie flew in to Detroit and rented a white Cadillac limousine that he really couldn't afford but he was damned if Papa wasn't going to have, "the best goin' out!" It was his way of dealing with his own overpowering grief. He arrived at our place and fell into my arms, sobbing like a child. At the service, he was barely able to finish a heart-felt, tear-filled eulogy.

Frank David's three elderly sisters, my aunts, flew in from Manitoba and Richie made it his mission, to chauffeur them in grand style from the airport and all day long, in the regal white coach. Theirs was the lead car in the funeral procession, and it was a fitting touch and fine tribute for a man we had loved, and who had loved us, so dearly.

Chapter Thirteen

"Half of what I say is meaningless

But I say it just to rest you Julia...

-John Lennon

Being married and raising kids consumed my life. With the demands and added expense I had to make better money. I started looking for a "day job." To a musician, this was a sign that music itself wasn't paying the bills and it was depressing. But I looked at it as a way to update my musical equipment, an area where I was way behind the times. And in my wife's eyes, at least I was trying. One of the first places I went was Home Depot where the interviewer asked me,

"So what makes you think you'd be qualified to work here?" and after thinking for a moment I replied,

"My father was a carpenter." I think the man marveled at my audacity or plain honesty but he hired me and I began my career in Hardware. I knew nothing about hardware and every day it was my terrifying nightmare that at any moment my secret would be discovered. Most customers knew more than I did and probably the line I used the most was,

"I don't know but I'll find out," at which the busy patrons would roll their eyes and look for someone else to help them. One thing I got pretty good at was giving directions. I'd walk the isles and take mental pictures, storing them for later use. One of the most inane policies that the higher-ups insisted on was saying hello to everyone we met, all day long. This included fellow employees and after a while, we'd be saying hello to each other a dozen times a day! It was ridiculous and completely insincere. Our customers weren't stupid. They knew it was designed to suck the money out of them. Believe it or not I lasted eleven months at that job until I couldn't take it any more.

I went back to music with renewed enthusiasm. A horrible day at playing music was better than the best day selling hardware! I started doing a solo act. I hadn't done that since the days back in high school when I joined the Folk Club and everybody had to perform solo as an initiation. It terrified me then and it still scared the bejesus out of me twenty years later but the thought of doing anything else frightened me more.

It occurred to me that by using my studio, I could create the 'band' and put them on tape, and then just play and sing along in a live situation. There were some real problems with that in the early days. The format then, was cassettes and after a while the tape would stretch and I'd no longer be in tune with the backup music. Sometimes the start of a song was fine and then halfway through...well it wasn't pretty. Another problem was acceptance. People just couldn't fathom what I was doing and some would say,

"Aw, he ain't singin'!" This would piss me off to no end, after all the freakin' hours I had spent practicing. But I got used to it and in time, people began to understand me. As a one-man-band, I could fit into the cracks where bigger bands or even duos wouldn't work. And I worked six nights a week. It was hard, my fingers were sore and sometimes I'd lose my voice, but it was pretty good dough.

Then came Karaoke.

Suddenly, everyone thought they were a singer and almost none of them were. To me, the only thing worse than a bad singer, was the idiot that encouraged him. Where on earth did the idea come from, that folks who never worked at it, never struggled about it, and who had no talent whatsoever, should get up on a stage and make such a God awful sound and be accepted so heartily? It was the sign of a society gone completely haywire. And now they were putting me out of work. At the height of the craze, people would pester me all night long,

"My sister is a singer," they'd say, "Everybody wants to hear her."

"I'm not Karaoke," I'd try to explain but they didn't want to hear it.

"Oh c'mon, don't be an asshole."

It would ruin my night. Fortunately, it passed. Thank God I had my studio.

Chapter Fourteen

"A diamond necklace played the pawn,

Hand in hand some drummed along,

To a handsome man and baton...

-Brian Wilson

1986

With the sale of my father's house I was able to expand my small basement recording facility. My wife looked forward to the extra income. My kids barely seemed to notice the folks coming and going. The word went out among musicians and songwriters that a reasonably priced, comfortable studio was close at hand and gradually I filled up my calendar. Strangers in our house at first, clients soon became familiar and in time, even close friends.

One such studio pal raved on to me about his younger brother's rap group.

"Oh man they goin' all the way," he swaggered. I hated rap music but since I desperately needed the income, I encouraged him to send them in. A few weeks later, two enterprising young boys showed up, both about 22. They brought with them, two overly vivacious, and yes, gorgeous ladies.

Two things became instantly obvious to me. The guys didn't know what they were doing... and the girls did. Contrary to what most people thought, it *did* require talent to perform rap correctly. Perhaps it couldn't be characterized as music but nevertheless there was a trick to doing it right. And as a producer, I was supposed to know what those tricks were. But these boys knew no tricks and had no talent whatsoever!

There I was, trying to make sense of the complete lunacy in the control room, while every opening of the door to the waiting room began to reveal two ladies becoming more naked by the minute!

Although I was raised a Mennonite I'm ashamed to say, I couldn't wait for the door to open again! I mean these blonde bombshells were hot with a capital H! It came out that the boys had stopped by the "titty bar" on the way to the studio, and had dazzled the off duty strippers into coming along to the "record company."

One floor above, in my sedate family home, my innocent nine-year-old Julia labored quietly over her homework, her fresh-faced brothers Michael and Jason competed on a computer game in the living room, and my dutiful wife Grace tidied the kitchen. Meanwhile, one floor below, it had become a house of porn! The girls were dancing in my waiting room, completely naked!

Seems the boys had outright lied to them about being "rap stars" but by the time they had arrived at the studio, they were all so high, it didn't matter anyway! The whole thing was a ruse to get the ladies to 'give it up!' They had been drinking, and other stuff too, and I began to wonder if the police weren't going to burst in at any moment! I prayed that no one in my family would suddenly decide to do laundry! I could just hear it,

"La-dee-dee, la-dee-da, Oh my God!" The night finally ended and I escaped unscathed.

One unexpected day, the following summer, Gracie suddenly stretched a pair of panties in my face and asked, "Do you know who belongs to these?" Oh boy.

There were also plenty of joyous times in the studio.

One Amish family sang in a barbershop style. They notified me that they might bring a few cheerleaders to the session and they weren't kidding. Half an hour before start time, three pickup trucks pulled up and Grandpa and Grandma and everyone on down, squeezed into the tiny control room to record and witness the goings-on. They reminded me of the people I had grown up with. There were perhaps twenty, gentle, Mennonite-types, all sitting quietly, some listening and I thought some probably praying. I had remembered to remove even remotely suggestive posters from my walls.

It all started so innocently. They sang gorgeous barber shop harmonies, praising their Lord Jesus, and after an entire afternoon of singing, fell back in their chairs, completely exhausted. However, there had been a mistake at the end of the line "where his body was laid," and I assured them, much to their relief, that I could erase the error by technical means and they wouldn't have to sing another note. I proceeded to forward and rewind over the line with my recording machine, stopping always after the word "*laid*." I deftly practiced doing this for a full five minutes before actually erasing, now only that auspicious word coming out, over and over.

Laid, z-z-o-o-o-p,

L*aid*, z-z-o-o-o-p was the only sound in the room.

Finally I got it! Everyone breathed easier but Grandpa said it out loud, "Thank God! I've never been *laid* so much in my whole life!"

The entire room exploded in one long fit of laughter! Sedate, conservative, Amish-type old ladies in shawls, their grown children, and young teenagers, all doubled over with laughter, tears streaming down cheeks. I gained a new appreciation for those folks in that magic moment. Even my kids came halfway down the stairs to see what was so funny! Grandpa seemed shocked by all the fuss but soon he was smiling about it too. It was perfect.

Talk about someone with great timing. Dale Williams, a trim, handsome Patrick Swayze look alike in his middle 50s, owned a lawn care business. After spraying our grass one day, the bare-chested, gentle soul in rubber boots happened to mention to me that he was a big band singer and he certainly was. Eventually cutting several albums with me, his giant, silky baritone voice would always stand out as my favorite. I loved him more than even Sinatra or any of the other great ones! He really and truly *was* one of the most remarkable vocalists I had ever heard and how he never surfaced in the music business was a complete mystery to me.

11 years my senior, Williams was like a friendly older brother and he could *make me laugh*. Things would happen in his life, that I found quite hilarious, and I would beg this unassuming man to recount his tales of woe, over and over again.

This was one of my favorites.

Over the years, he had developed a fondness for going to the nudist camps. There was nothing salacious about it. He simply enjoyed the freedom of being around people that had nothing to hide, and he in turn would hide nothing. It had not been easy at first. Walking stark naked among other stark naked folks, had taken a little getting used to. He was a shy, modest man and in the early days, had always worn shorts. Then came the day he had been hired to perform as a DJ and vocalist at a nudist resort function in Northern Michigan. Arriving early to set up, the rugged, 50-year-old suddenly had plenty of time to spare on a warm summer day. He decided to take a walk.

Finally, feeling safe, he courageously peeled off his clothes for the first time, setting them on a log, experiencing the complete freedom all nudists come to feel. Swinging merrily among the pines, wearing nothing but tennis shoes, he came to a lake and noticed several canoes tied to a dock. Wondering if the crafts were for anyone's use, he saw two women, also nude, sitting on some lawn chairs nearby. He knew this would be his first real test so with a deep breath, he approached, and stood dangling before them.

"Excuse me," he began, but before he could say any more, one of the women exclaimed, "Dale Williams, we know you!"

He was several hundred miles away from home and not a soul should have known him. It was the last place on earth he expected to be recognized, and the last condition he expected to be in, at the moment of said recognition!

"We see you all the time in Belleville," the lady continued, and now he wished with all his heart that he had brought a towel. As he stood there with a forced smile in stuttered conversation, his cover blown, he witnessed his own initiation into the world of naked.

Then there was Ernie...

Chapter Fifteen

"People are strange, when you're a stranger..."

-The Doors.

Ernie and his wheelchair brigade had already been banished from several local malls for harassing women. He would just say whatever popped into his head and sometimes it was not taken in the spirit it was delivered.

"Hey, you'd sure look good naked in those shoes," he might say to a startled housewife passing by. When he would verbalize things like that, he actually meant them. In his mind he was complimenting. Of course security would be called. They didn't understand that it was just his mensa brain trying desperately to get out of his body. I would think back to the summer day in 1985, when I spoke to him for the first time. The voice on the other end was slow and deliberate and I knew from the sound my mother had made, that I was speaking to a person of handicap.

"I'm a rock--and roller like you, man. Uh--I saw you at the bar-- uh--you were great, man. I was wondering--if I could--make an album--at your studio?"

In his mind, he was the next 'big thing.' Just a few years earlier at the age of 17, he was taking his drummer home from their band rehearsal. They were traveling at a low rate of speed. Their car hit some loose gravel, and then a cement culvert. It was a freak accident. Though his friend walked away, Ernie the budding guitar player and genius songwriter did not. In coma for 6 months, doctors said he might never walk, or talk, again. A closed head injury affected his motor skills and speech.

It was a parent's worst nightmare.

But Ernie got a little better. Over the years he regained some use of his arms and could actually stand, albeit very slowly and carefully. And he certainly could talk! When I met him for the first time I was amazed at his cutting edge creative ideas!

"Let me be your hands and you just sing and produce the sessions," I reasoned with the barrel-chested, Mel Gibson look-a-like, and we rolled up our sleeves and went to work. It would take the new rock star 10 minutes to walk the 20 feet to the vocal booth, get positioned, and strap on the headphones, but he did it! His breathing was labored but if he got a good lung full of air, he could sing or talk 4 or 5 words at a stretch. It didn't matter to him; he was rockin' and rollin' again!

When Richie heard the tracks, with enthusiasm he said,

"It's no less edgy than the stuff here on the left coast, and that stuff is selling like crazy!"

I would get frustrated at some of the wackiness of the music but then would try to remember why he was there and would just let go. I imagined what it would have been like to be Salvador Dali's instructor! Ernie became the most productive of all the acts at my studio, releasing four, different, full-blown CDs in less than three years! He pressed and sold or gave away, at least 200 copies of each! His albums looked and for the most part, sounded just like the ones in the record stores.

I had been blessed with being able to walk, run, dance, sing, make-love; move about. What did I have to be sad about? Ernie had the miraculous gift of excelling in the prison in which he found himself.

We developed a strong friendship. I loved the guy.

One day some 2 years into our relationship, he called me to come see his new guitar. As I coveted the gorgeous, pure white, American Fender Stratocaster reverently, my friend crowed,

"It's yours--and I won't--take no--for an answer!"

I was stunned at the love and generosity of this kind soul, but already knew I couldn't accept such a gift, worth several thousand dollars, until his father took me aside and said,

"Please John. He will be *crushed* if you don't accept it."

I couldn't believe it! At first I didn't even feel worthy of picking up the instrument. Eventually, it became the only guitar I would use on stage and unlike others, stayed miraculously in tune, even over night! Guitars never stay in tune like this one did. Unbelievably, I had my white Strat! It would *never* be less than 20 feet from me.

Through all the years I'd known him, my handicapped friend had always talked about his dream of going to California. Since he couldn't travel alone, he offered to pay for my entire trip if I would accompany him! Again it was his father who insisted and a few months later, with my wife's blessing, the two of us found ourselves on a 747, winging our way to Hollywood. One of the first things my pal asked me was,

"Do you think--there will be-- hookers at our--hotel?"

I assured him there would be and he relaxed and closed his eyes.

We had booked 2 rooms at the famous Roosevelt in the heart of the city, the setting for hundreds of motion pictures over the years. Everyone from Charlie Chaplin to David Foster had produced films here and it just so happened that a movie called Club Land was being filmed during our stay. On a daily basis my wheel-chaired protégé and I, would be on the elevators with cast and crew. Never shy, and with nothing to lose, Ernie would flirt with the young female star of the movie, while she waited to shoot her next scene.

"Hey sweetie--want to--go for--eh--ride?" He'd invite from his chair, carefully pronouncing the long 'a.' She would giggle and soon he'd have her phone number!

Sometimes I would find myself in the uncomfortable position of being the 'responsible adult.' It was warm and sunny on the Universal Studios tour. There were star-look-a-likes everywhere. As I wheeled my cohort past a saloon porch hosted by a beckoning Mae West, Ernie asked to be pushed up close so he could speak to her. I didn't see any harm in that so I did as requested and then stepped back to snap a photo. Everything was fine until the buxom woman in the low-cut gown leaned forward and cooed her Hollywood bit,

"Why don't you come up and see me sometime, big boy?" That was all he needed to hear.

He lunged forward from his wheelchair, as though he had never been crippled, and buried his head in her breasts, jiggling vigorously from side to side! Horrified, I rushed to the scene and began apologizing profusely, pulling the perpetrator back. She stopped me however, and insisted it was all right and continued to speak gently to him. She probably thought he was retarded, but he certainly wasn't! He was just horny!

All the way back to the hotel, I tried to lecture my friend about the do's and don'ts of vacationing but had to stay behind the wheelchair and keep my laughter suppressed. I thought it had been a scream, his hair sticking up; glasses half-cocked on his face, from his frantic 'titty-dive!'

At every corner, free tickets were being given away for the many TV shows that taped every day in Hollywood. Oh this was pretty cool.

"*Dharma and Greg*!" one would shout, while another beckoned,

"*Friends*!" And it was a tough decision but Ernie had a social consciousness. He wanted Politically Incorrect, which was filmed 'live' as it happened.

The large group we found ourselves with, was 'herded' silently up elevators in the CBS building, and finally, quietly seated in a cold, dark studio. They placed my excited friend's chair on the main floor, giving full deference to the handicap and showing them respect, with me one level up but directly behind... within striking distance. Ten minutes before show time, Bill Maher came out to warm up the crowd and asked if there were any questions. I froze as Ernie's hand immediately shot up!

Please God, let it be something normal, I prayed.

"I under—stand Penthouse's Bob Guccione—has—a lot of—shoes in—his closet." The audience roared at the puzzled look on Maher's face. And then to all of our delights, Ernie and Bill Maher proceeded to banter back and forth on the subject for the next five minutes! Boy, talk about an otherworldly experience. Finally, the host lowered his eyes, drew a bead on my friend, and with a wink said,

"That'll be enough out of you young man!" It brought down the house. I was real sorry that it didn't make it to air and I'll bet the producers were too. I relaxed and thought, 'Way to go Ernie.'

Being taken to the titty bar was practically all my traveling companion talked about. I didn't like those places but conceded that in his shoes, I might want to do the very same thing. I wondered what I would say to his dad if he ever found out I took him there!

"*You took him where?*"

I paid, then wheeled the anticipating lad passed the shifty-looking 'security guard' and into the dark back room where 3 gorgeous, scantily-clad beauties began immediately to fawn over him, stroking his hair, and spoiling him.

"You lookin' for a good time baby?" I figured it would take a steel brush to wipe the smile off that face! He would certainly believe every word they said about him, to his grave!

"That was--eh--blast," he said as I wheeled him back to the hotel. I found out a few weeks later, that the following day at the Roosevelt, Ernie actually picked a hooker up from the street and brought her to his room!

"You could have been robbed, or worse," I chastised him. But I understood that he had just wanted a few minutes of fun, and I thought, why not? Again I pictured his dad, hands on hips, asking incredulously,

"You let him do what?"

Chapter Sixteen

"This old heart of mine, been broke a thousand times..."

-The Isley Brothers

1988

From the time I was 15 and playing with the Y-Knotts I dreamed about making it big. You know how that is. Sometimes you just think you're 'all that' and it drives you forward. I really believed I was good enough for the big time and I focused all my energies, through all the years, trying to get there. It meant thousands of hours of practice, writing songs, rejecting ideas, accepting others, being rejected; it was dedication of the highest degree. But I loved it. It was both work and hobby. I had no interest in anything else. There was one time when I came so deliciously close to success, I almost reached out and touched it.

Gary was Warren Beatty. He had the same sleepy look on his face, at all times. He had perfect hair, longish, a little curly and swept back, and girls thought he was a dreamboat. But his calm, self-effacing exterior belied a monster talent. So much so that there would come a day, he would be asked to work for the rap artist Eminem's company! The nearest I ever came to big time recording success was during the days I collaborated with Gary.

He told me about his four-track basement studio and I was totally impressed. In 1972, no one that I knew of had four tracks in their basement! We began writing songs together and building up quite an extensive catalogue over the years. I would drive from Kingsville to his home in Detroit and spend a few days and we'd lock ourselves in the studio and create. It was a perfect collaboration and a solid friendship.

In the eighties, Gary opened a full service recording studio on the east side of Detroit, catering to a variety of recording stars including some that were signed to major labels. He was a knowledgeable producer and engineer and his state-of-the-art facility grew in reputation. It became difficult for me to get him to find time to write and record with me! But I didn't give up.

In fact, I took a job as janitor, coffee maker, and backup engineer just so I could be around the studio. Gracie wasn't too crazy about it because I'd be gone from sunrise to sunset and wouldn't bring home any money except whatever the studio generated in petty cash. My satisfaction level was way up. Just by being available, I wound up playing guitar and violin for dozens of producers and projects from around the world. I even got my name in some of the credits!

But meanwhile, all I wanted to do was record the stuff that Gary and I had written. It was fresh and exciting and we would produce it to compete with anything that was out there. If only we could get a break.

The break came in 1988 in the form of Ken Simpson. He came to Gary looking for a job and my friend hired him on the spot. Who wouldn't with his qualifications? His credits included Marvin Gaye and Stevie Wonder. At Motown, he had been in charge of recording all the string and horn sessions! But Motown had moved to LA and Ken had kids in Detroit and wanted to stay there. Just by virtue of him being at our studio, the business exploded! Now, huge stars and known producers were coming through our doors and we were cutting hit records. I became very close with Ken and one day he said to me,

"You and Gary have some brilliant stuff in the can but you need a recognizable tune to introduce yourself to radio programmers. Why don't you make a new version of This Old Heart of Mine?"

I wondered about the wisdom of cutting this classic Four Tops tune but knew better than to question a man of his experience so I rolled up my sleeves and went to work. Every spare moment I had, I was at the piano, building the ideas for the song. Gary would arrive at the studio early in the morning, all sleepy-eyed, and I'd already be at work.

"Not yet," Ken would say, as I would eagerly show him that I was ready to begin recording the song. It was driving me crazy to have to wait so long. Then finally one morning as my wise mentor prepared for a coming session, he suddenly said,

"Let's lay it down!"

"What, without a band? How?" I asked. He rolled the tape machine and while it was in record mode, scurried out to the drum booth, grabbed the sticks, and began playing the sweetest groove I had ever heard! It was definitely a Motown feeling and he was as solid as a drum machine. I didn't even know Ken played drums but on that tune, he grooved like the best drummers in town! Instinctively I ran to the keyboard and counted us in,

"One, two, three...and with that we swung into the greatest feeling track I had ever played. Adding instruments over the next few days was easy for Gary and me because the initial track was so good. We knew we had a very strong tune but how strong?

Because Ken was so well known, everybody that was anybody would come around the studio, on a regular basis. One day, Scott Regal, a DJ that I remembered being on C K R W and who now was doing A & R for a new record company out of New York called Private Stock, sauntered in and I heard Ken say,

"Just sit right there Scott, and don't move. I want you to hear something," and with that he played our finished track through the rumbling speakers. Before the first chorus even hit, Scott was on his feet screaming,

"That's it, that's it! It's a smash!" And I was in heaven.

From there, things jumped off pretty quickly. Scott took the track to his boss in New York, and three weeks later, we were on the radio with a single record deal and an album deal in the works! Our version of This Old Heart of Mine became top-ten-requested on stations in California and New York. The name of our recording band was The Shivers and since no one around Detroit knew it was my band, I couldn't enjoy the excitement with any one except my family. I had a record on the radio, nation-wide, and none of my peers knew!

As it had happened with a band I'd been in back in the sixties, the excitement lasted for about two months and then one day the phone rang in the studio. Ken hung it up slowly and his tired red eyes said it all,

"Private Stock has gone bankrupt." I couldn't believe my ears. This one really hurt. I was so sure, we were all sure, that this time, it was going to be big time success. I drove home in shock, went down to my crying room and once again, shed some good tears.

Chapter Seventeen

"The road is long, with many a winding turn..."

-The Hollies.

1990

For some mysterious reason, around the time I turned forty, a nagging curiosity about my past began to haunt me. What led to my adoption? Who were my 'real' parents, and why did they have to give me up? I imagined so many things. My Mom, Dad and Frances had always told me when I was a kid that my birth parents were "trying to get you back!"

"You're not to talk or go anywhere with strangers," my mother would warn, emphatically.

When I became an adult I began to suspect that it had all been a ruse, designed to make me feel wanted, and a brilliant one at that.

"I'm really not sure John," my sister would finally concede years later, when we were both adults.

Now I was ready to know the truth. It took almost a year but finally a notice came in the mail that the Ontario Adoption Search's computer had drawn a match! Although I expected it might, what with my birth folks *supposedly* looking for me all those years, it was still a shock. I fantasized about a tearful TV reunion, my aged, bedraggled parents on the cushy sofa, clutching hands and pleading,

"Oprah, we made a terrible mistake in giving John up and we just hope and pray he can forgive us now."

And of course on national TV, who wouldn't!

But the computer said it was a brother, not a parent.

Holy Shit! I hadn't even thought of *that* possibility! I wondered what my newfound sibling would be like. Would he be sweet or gruff, brilliant or dull, younger or older?

I stared at the phone for several agonizing minutes, wondering if curiosity was going to kill this cat. After all, he could have been a CEO or he could have been in prison! It was like standing on a high diving platform, not sure of the water's depth below. Finally, deliberately, I dialed the Eastern Canadian number and after two rings a voice that sounded very much like my own answered,

"Hello?"

Then I heard myself say,

"This is your brother John calling."

"Hi Bro, this is Joe."

The voice on the other end began to unleash a lifetime of news over the next 30 minutes. He was two years older than me. Great, just what I needed. I would have maybe liked to be the *older* brother in this situation. Other than that, the similarities were astounding!

"I'm a musician, a guitarist, and I've played in bands since I was in high school."

My God, just like me!

"I was in a group that was signed to a major label but we just didn't have the right song."

Oh boy.

"I've just released a solo album and I'm in the process of pitching it to some labels."

Now I felt as though I was talking to myself and I began to squirm in my chair. My brother had searched for our birth family like a private investigator for 20 years. For some reason, it had been vitally important to him, much more so than me.

"When I finally found our mother 'eh..." and as his, already familiar voice continued the spell, he now had my complete attention, as I paced back and forth helplessly throughout the house on the cordless phone.

"...She kinda' reluctantly invited me to meet her present family in British Columbia. It was 5000 miles but I went, and after a quick 24 hour visit, during which time I met our brother Bill, also a musician..."

At this point I began to feel completely un-unique. I was already convinced that I had made a terrible mistake and wished I could just turn back the hands of time one hour.

"...I found out, he's a hell of a bass player!"

Good God, I thought. We've got a whole fucking band in the family! As Joe unraveled the story, I couldn't believe what I was hearing. Then came the final blow.

"When I told Mother *you* had surfaced, she *freaked*."

There it was. It was laughable now and I shook my head at all of it, in abject amazement. Be careful what you wish for I thought.

"No one in her family knew about you, *you* were the deep dark secret!" Joe continued, almost gleefully it seemed to me now.

I thought about how terrified the woman must be, thinking that a mistake she had made 40 years ago could come back to haunt her at any moment! I could never do that in a million years. My curiosity had been more than satisfied with what I had discovered and I was left with a feeling that this had been an activity I should never have dallied in. It was almost more than I could bear.

"Just tell her I'm alright and we'll let it go at that," I insisted, hiding my disappointment. It was rather ironic for me to have wanted to unlock so much, and yet to have found *way* too much!

Joe seemed like a good guy. By the time three weeks of reminiscing by phone went by, we felt comfortable enough to have a meeting in the town where Joe grew up, St. Catherine's, Ontario. It meant a 3-hour journey for me and three times that for him but at least we were actually going to meet face to face!

Arriving early, I tried to think of creative ways to make the Motel 6's bare walls seem more inviting but there was not much to be done with one horrible painting. Since I had brought nothing but my clothes and violin, it was hopeless. The drab, grey room with the noisy, overactive radiator mirrored my own helplessness at my seemingly irreversible situation.

Finally, there was a knock at the door and there stood Joe, looking like a brother would, that was two years older. It was like a Twilight Zone episode, as surreal as looking out the airplane window at 30,000 feet and seeing someone on the wing! He was an inch shorter, a pound or two heavier, but had many of the same facial features as me. That he was my brother was without question. I thought it was probably like looking in a mirror two years down the road, and that was a very strange feeling indeed!

We hugged cordially, slapping each other's back.

"Nice to finally meet you," he said enthusiastically.

"Yeah, likewise," I tried to sound as excited, but inside, I just wasn't. What the hell was wrong with me?

For the next four hours the room was filled with the sounds of vibrating acoustic rock and blues jams as Joe fingered brilliant guitar and I sawed madly away on my fiddle. He was one of the best pickers I had ever heard although very much into his own playing. It was a good jam but I was glad when it was over. I just wasn't ready to have an older brother.

Perhaps if we hadn't lived 2000 miles away from each other, things might have been different. We talked once a year after that and the distance between us was obvious. Eventually, we lost touch and I always felt a little guilty because I didn't regret it.

Chapter Eighteen

"Go to Hawaii, Hawaii, straight to Hawaii,

Oh do you, wanna' come along with me..."

-The Beach Boys.

1992

Middle aging was hard for me. It really bugged me that at the age of 42, I hadn't had any tangible success and that I was still the same struggling musician that I had always been, still playing in smoky taverns. My demo tapes to record labels came back unopened or rejected and none of my studio clients were having any luck either. I hadn't made enough money to set any aside for old age, and the way I was thinking then; unless something big happened in my career, I was going to be screwed. Winters made things worse. A depression would set in that made me miserable and angry. For my poor wife Gracie my frustration became as predictable as clockwork each year starting around November.

"Honey, let's just sell the house and go to Florida and be done with this weather," I would plead.

"Well then, we'll lose money and be in more debt trying to buy a new one there, that's not even as nice as the one we have *now*! *And*, you'll have lost all your studio clients."

I always gave up because when it came to common sense, she seemed to have more of it than me. Years later I would regret not taking a firmer stand on that *one* issue.

One day in the dead of 1992's brutal winter, she came home excitedly from work saying,

"I just heard about a contest on the radio and the grand prize is a trip to Hawaii!"

I immediately pooh-poohed the idea. After all the years and expense of carefully submitting tapes and sending them to people I would never hear from, I was pissed off and fed up.

"No one ever wins those things, least of all me," I grumbled. By this time in my life I was so overwhelmed with failure that not doing anything, felt safe. In my fantasy world, I was still good. Out of breath, she continued,

"No listen. All you have to do is write a jingle with '96.2 and Bud Lite' somewhere in the lyrics!"

Well, I began to think, if I just do it and show her that it can't happen, maybe she will understand why I feel the way I do! So, more to prove a point than anything else, I went downstairs to my studio, rolled up my sleeves, made a funky drum and bass line, added harmonies, and came up with a cute little song called "96.2 and Bud Lite!" It took only three hours. I didn't think it was very original but it was exactly what was asked for in the contest.

"You're going to win!" she gasped quite convincingly when she heard it for the first time. Although it was oddly infectious, to me, I was still going to be able to say, "I told you so," at the end of it all.

Three weeks later, and unbelievably to me in a radio market as big as Detroit's, I had been chosen one of 5 semi-finalists! It was awesome, just being in the running for something and I conceded to my lovely lady that maybe she had been right after all. At last, a little validation had come my way although at this point, I had no delusions of winning.

Then came the icy winter morning at 6 am, as I sat in an easy chair in a half-sleep state, radio down low, and heard the jock say,

"Right after this, we'll interview the winner of our, 'Sing Your Way to Paradise' contest."

Some lucky dog goin' 'ta Hawaii, I thought, as I stared at the huge icicles hanging outside from the eaves, scratching my dry skin, wondering if I even had a 'next move' for the music business.

Suddenly the phone rang and it scared the shit out of me! Who could be calling at this hour I actually wondered? Realizing my family was accounted for, I answered tentatively,

"Hello?" The voice on the line was jazzed.

"Hello John, this is 96.2 and you and a friend are going to Hawaii!" I couldn't believe it! I had never won anything like this! After the announcer and his sidekick joked with me a while, they signed off, giving me instructions on where to pick up the tickets. My wife and daughter had heard the commotion and now we all crowded together, Gracie chanting,

"We're going to Hawaii, I told you, I told you!"

I guess she told me.

At my club that night, the word had spread and folks that had heard me win on the air gave me a, "way to go." As a one-man-band playing in the corner of a smoky, small-time bar for what seemed like forever, I would usually get on stage each night of my life, feeling like a real nobody. It was such a relief, to finally get some kind of recognition, even if it was just a silly contest.

Three months later, and still quite unbelievably to me, Grace and I were jetting to Paradise and what I thought was finally going to be a brighter future.

I thought that; because I had won a jingle contest on the biggest FM station in Detroit, it would somehow jump-start my career but it had no such effect. Not once at the radio station, when I picked up my tickets, or in Hawaii, did anyone so much as inquire about my work. I was actually shocked about this. When we had checked in at our hotel on Maui, I had expected a phalanx of suit-types to come out and say,

"So you're the contest winner. We've been expecting you!"

Instead, I excitedly began to tell the clerk about everything that had happened when, unimpressed, she looked up from her work and smilingly said,

"Our hotel is full of contest-winners tonight sir!"

And just like that, my ego returned to its familiar back seat. It really had been just a silly radio promotion after all and it was time I knew it. More for Gracie than anyone else, I had hoped for something different. She had worked so hard for so many years, raising three beautiful children while working 40-hour jobs she sometimes hated. I wanted her to be able to take it easy and enjoy life while I made the good income... Not this time. Good grief, what do I have to do, I wondered?

Chapter Nineteen

"I'm a travelin' man and I've made a lot of stops,

All over the world..."

-Ricky Nelson.

1995

My wife and I started to grow apart. Money, or rather the lack of it, was at the root. My own unhappiness certainly played a part. Also, she was intelligent, responsible, and business-like and I was still the same, easy-going artist-type that I had always been, that didn't pay attention to finances. Around Detroit there were fewer places to perform now, fewer nights, and the cost of gear kept increasing. A music career didn't come cheap.

Everything seemed to be put on hold the summer that Gracie's sister Joan and her husband took us on a 3-week tour of Europe!

"Europe?" I gasped excitedly when my wife had told me the news. It was a far away land on the Travel Channel but certainly not some place I thought I would *ever* get to visit! The first thing that I thought of was, how am I going to stand that length of time without a guitar? I was practicing every day now and 3 weeks was an eternity *not* to practice. But then I remembered I had just completed my CD of violin instrumental music and, what with America beginning to go 'rap'-crazy, maybe

I'd stand a better chance of finding acceptance for it in Europe where they were much more open to new ideas. I decided to embrace the whole thing and once again felt a spark of hope for my sagging career.

I also truly loved my wife's family and looked forward to spending quality time with them. They were genuine folks. But most importantly, I hoped the trip would give my troubled marriage a boost. By this time, Gracie and I were speaking only in terse, necessary sentences, and even our kids could tell, there was something wrong. We had made the same mistake many couples make of not setting enough time aside for each other, but there was something else. The kids were grown and we had begun to sense that our chemistry was running out.

The whole Europe trip could have filled a book. It was one fabulous sensory experience after another. There were hundreds of firsts on this adventure. From running out of gas deep in the heart of troubled Yugoslavia to dining with a Count and Countess in their castle in the south of France, every day was a non-stop, wild and wacky adventure. But at the end of each night, Gracie and I still went to sleep on our own side of the bed. Floating serenely over the Loire Valley in a hot air balloon on a gentle, breezy summer day, it should have been a sight romantic enough to mend any fences but my wife kept her distance. When I would try to put my arm around her, she'd find any excuse to break away.

My spirit was broken.

England was our last stop. Except for the castle stay, the four of us had done everything pretty much on a shoestring, but here in London we stayed in a private hotel across from beautiful Hyde Park, that famous place of Jack The Ripper lore, where the Queen's attendants gave her horses their daily run. The small but well-staffed accommodations had been host to the rock artist Sting, and then The Rolling Stones, just a year before and my in-laws had picked it because of the appeal it would have for me. Sleeping in the same bed as Mick Jagger would have to be a good omen I thought, considering it was here that I would take a day off to promote my album.

I was terrified and I knew the chances were slim, but I rolled up my sleeves and went to it the best I knew how. I would never have another opportunity like this. While the others were on their way to Buckingham Palace for a tour I wished I could have taken, I took a crash course in double-decker busing from the kind hotel concierge, and hit the streets. I was determined to find *someone* that could *hear* my music. The task was compounded by the fact that I was a stranger in a strange land. The English language as spoken by people from England, was barely understandable to me, a Canadian for Pete's sake!

Unlike New York, L.A. or Nashville, the companies were spread far and wide around the city and it took all day of hopping on and off of timed buses. And though

I was treated cordially everywhere, there wasn't much interest in instrumental music that wasn't *cutting edge*, in the 90s sense. Rap music had begun to erode common sense here too. Nevertheless, I left my material with each secretary and prayed for a miracle.

I had one final stop to make and that was at EMI, located in the same building as the Beatles' Abbey Road Studios. Weary of the bus, and with just enough money left, I hailed one of London's 19,000 Hansom cabs, complete with dashing uniformed, gentleman driver, and 45 minutes later, we pulled up in front of one of the most famous structures in the entire world. I stared in awe at the Abbey Road sign. Once inside, I pleaded my case with yet another polite, understanding secretary, who had nothing promising to tell me.

"We'll ring you up love, if we're interested," she tried to assure, her lovely accent making me smile. I was quite familiar now, with the tone. As I turned to leave, I almost crashed head to head with a dapper gentleman in a gray tweed suit. Oh my God, I gasped to myself! It was Sir George Martin, producer of the Beatles! This was as famous a face in the music business as there was. Without him, there probably would have been no *Beatles,* as we knew them!

"Oh, sorry!"

"Oh no, pardon me!" we said to each other as I gathered myself and went past. I had spoken to George Martin! It had all happened so fast, I hadn't time to think! All the way home and for the rest of my days I would wish that I had gotten down on bended knee, right there in the busy lobby and first of all, kissed the man's feet and secondly, begged him to listen to my CD! But then, that probably happened to the poor soul every day! As I glanced back over my shoulder I knew I was witnessing yet another missed opportunity.

The wise old chauffer, who had knowingly waited across the street, gave me some perspective.

"You were luckiah than mewst suh," he comforted through his handle bar moustache in a soft voice as we conversed by rear view mirror on the way back to the hotel, as I stared glumly out the window at passing London.

"Even people who live heah don't get a Sir George Mah-tin sighting!" Yes I was sure that was true.

The whole Europe trip, despite my dissolving marriage, had been an experience that I would treasure forever. In a few months, I would receive the obligatory refusal letters from all the labels I had been to see. They were the typical let-'em-down-easy ones:

We loved your submission. We're sorry, but it's not what we're looking for at this time. Please try again.

I had been submitting demo tapes wherever and whenever I had gotten a lead, for 25 years and now I had enough rejection letters to paper one entire wall of my studio. It made a great collage. I wanted my clients to know that rejection was inevitable, and I wanted my children to know that I had tried. The 'wall,' was my way of putting some kind of positive spin on the "no's" I had received for all the years. In my own small way, I was giving one last finger to the music business. I would never submit to anyone, ever again.

For three weeks, Gracie and I had been on hold. Now, back home, the cold silences and sarcastic innuendos returned. Couples falling out of love are sometimes not very nice people. The pain was too deep. It became obvious that both of us needed to escape. I just wanted out so I let her have everything. The entire divorce cost 120 dollars. Attorney friends would tell me that after 20 years of marriage, I was entitled to half. But it would have meant selling the place where my kids had made their memories. Freedom had its price.

So now for the first time in my life, I felt as though I had lost everything, my parents, best friend, children, career, and the one person that had promised to love me forever. If not for my music, I might have lost my mind.

I rented the only thing I could afford, a modest apartment big enough to house my studio, above a noisy air conditioning business, sharing it with the displaced family cats, Tonto and Tigger. I was terrified, but my biggest fear by far, was losing the love and respect of my children.

My boys lived nearby and my daughter was starting university in Ann Arbor, only a half hour away, and though our weekly communication assured me that they still loved me, two agonizing years, punctuated by frequent uncontrollable tears, crawled by. It was a divorce I had wanted and yet still, I felt a deep inner sadness and despaired that my life was a complete failure.

Chapter Twenty

"Lady in red, is dancing with me

There's nobody here, just you and me..."

-Chris Deburgh

During the next five years I did what most divorced people do... I made mistakes. At one point I fell head over heels in love with Juanita, a gorgeous girl fifteen years younger than me and was all set to give her my heart until the day she introduced me to her boyfriend, a handsome, successful Detroit radio producer and author. I groused for a few weeks after that until the day, the local News at Noon announced that a woman had been caught taking men to the altar and leaving them there and charges were to be filed. Lo and behold, it was my Juanita!

I believed in love and I guess you could say I was a hopeless romantic. Everyone said that I should give it time before jumping into a relationship, but I just couldn't. It had been an eternity since I had walked along the beach, held hands, looked into someone's eyes, and felt love.

I was ready.

Joanne was sitting in my audience one night, at a pizza place I was playing. She had pretty red hair, full lips, and wore a red dress, and when I played The Lady in Red for her; well, it's an unfair advantage singers have. They can charm almost any one by playing the right song at the right time!

You would never have known by looking at her as pretty as she was, that she was a Michigan State Police Sergeant! I couldn't believe I was dating a cop. It actually came in handy on a number of occasions. I got out of three tickets while I was dating her, twice when she was in the car with me, and once when she was in the car behind me. It was an awesome feeling to watch her "tin" the officer and witness his entire mood change.

"Okay, no problem. Just watch your speed next time sir," and we'd be on our way!

"I'd sure hate to get picked up by the *fuzz*," I'd quip and she'd laugh. Cops have a great sense of humor. It's what allows them to do the kind of job they have to do.

For my birthday, my daughter gave me two tickets to see the Beach Boys at the Michigan State Fair. Joanne and I made a day of it, anticipating the group's joyous music to come that evening. It was the music that had hit me emotionally during my teens. It was the music I still played loudly when no one else was around. We found our seats with plenty of time to spare and heard the announcer say,

"Place your bids now for charity and have a chance to meet The Beach Boys!" I looked at Joanne, my mouth wide open. Oh this was something. I ran to the auction table and placed my bid at sixty dollars, thinking I had it in the bag. In no time at all, the bids were at two hundred dollars and I despaired that I would miss my one chance in life to thank the boys for all they had meant to me.

"I'll pay half," sweet Joanne said, sensing my oncoming sadness. Back I ran with twice the buying power and this time I got it...at two hundred and fifty bucks! This was all the money I had available and hers too. But we were going to meet the Beach Boys!

By flashlight we were escorted, through backstage doors, past travel trailers, and into a large room where members of the backup band were singing harmonies and warming up their voices. This was really cool for me to see.

"Wait here," the man said and disappeared with his flashlight as we watched intently while the guys did their thing. There wasn't anything they played on this tour; no harmony they sang that I couldn't have done easily as well, and without even a rehearsal. I could have jumped up on the stage and fit in, almost without being noticed. I knew the material that well.

"One of our band members has taken ill. Is there anyone in the house that knows the songs?"

"I do, I do!" It was a little fantasy of mine.

Seconds later, around the corner just as casual as could be, came Mike Love and Bruce Johnson from the band.

"Hey thanks for donating to the good cause," I heard Love's voice say and I couldn't believe we were now having a conversation with my childhood heroes. I thought about Corey and the pact that we had made, that someday we'd meet The Beach Boys, and here I was.

"Thanks for all the great music guys," was all I could think of saying and after a quick photo, Joanne and I standing in between them, it was over. Numbly, we began to return to our seats when a voice rang out,

"Hey Sarg!" We turned to see two Michigan State Police officers who were working backstage security. Both had served under Joanne!

"Shit!" she whispered. We both realized in that instant that we could have met the band for *free*!

Chapter Twenty-One

"Mother-mother Ocean,

I have heard you call,

Wanted to sail upon your waters,

Since I was three feet tall..."

-Jimmy Buffett

2003

The smoke in Dandy's was now a visible blue haze. The sharpness of it was like a smelling salt. Here I was back in the present moment, awakened by a customer's voice,

"Play somethin' fast will ya?"

I had really been daydreaming. The three oldsters that had taken a tumble earlier had long since taken a cab home. My career was non existent. My personal life was empty. Joanne and I had parted as friends. I felt useless and worthless. I wanted to be in Florida but was afraid to leave familiar surroundings. Yet for years I had felt something calling me there.

I had reached the bottom. I was drinking every night, even though I didn't even like the taste. I just wanted to numb everything. Then, out of the blue, a miracle happened.

I had always liked and respected my friend Dale. What a nice guy he was. He drove the girls crazy when he sang because, not only did he sound like a younger and hipper Frank Sinatra, but he had this, deep-toned, smooth big-band voice that I and everyone else absolutely and unequivocally, adored. As a recording engineer I recorded him dozens of times but we were friends for twenty years before either of us thought of putting our two styles together.

Around the time I turned fifty I began preparing a Jimmy Buffett act. I figured if I had enough Buffett tunes I could go to Florida and work! Then finally, I would be free of the bitter mid-western winters that had depressed me for so long! And I also thought, if I'm destined to be playing in bars, let me at least play where it's warm and fun.

One nasty winter morning as I was talking from my mobile home near Ann Arbor, Michigan to the owner of the Dearborn Pub about a job he had hired me for, these words came out of my mouth.

"What would you think if I brought along this friend of mine that does Sinatra? Could you afford a little extra?"

I was sure he would say no but instead, I heard,

"Sure, let's try it. What are you going to call it?"

Good Lord, are we actually going to do this? I thought to myself. I hadn't even thought of a name. Without thinking I replied,

"Uh, *When Buffett Meets Sinatra*!"

I had no idea where the name came from but what a blessing it turned out to be. We combined our two styles, Dale performing a Sinatra tune, followed by me doing a Buffett song, and back and forth we went, all night long. From the very first set we ever did together, there was a magical 'something' that touched our audiences. Yes we were borrowing from two great artists but we never did so un-respectfully. If anything, those artists should be flattered, we did them proud. Folks told us so.

On a Monday night in football season, we started our auspicious duo. In 4 weeks there were lines at the door. In 8 weeks, folks were arriving 2 hours early just to save seats. In 12, the Dearborn News showed up and reviewed us! It was the nuttiest thing I had ever been involved with, and I simply couldn't explain it.

"Dale, what would you think if we went to Florida and tried to get some work there?" I casually asked my partner one day.

"Heck yeah, let's go!" was his surprise response, and in the days and weeks that followed, we began to formulate a plan.

We would save up enough money to last for three weeks in St. Petersburg and play anywhere and everywhere, anyone would listen. We took the time off in Michigan, made the trip together with all our gear in my mini-van and when the day came in April of 2003 for us to play our first audition at a cute little beach place called Philthy Phil's, we were *so* excited.

We arrived early in the afternoon to set up. It was a warm Florida day as we moved our gear up the long staircase and began setting up the speakers in the corner of the rooftop bar. The view from there was spectacular! Boats of every description cruised lazily up and down the intra-coastal waterway that stretched before us only yards away. Beautiful herons and egrets drifted overhead. Halfway through our set that normally moved at a breakneck pace, Dale paused between songs, looked at me and whispered off-mike,

"Oh my God, can you believe this?"

I really couldn't. I thought about my days at Cedar Beach as a teenager, watching the seagulls spin off the approaching sail-craft and I felt as lucky as the guy that had just hit the Lotto. I felt every cell in my body changing.

Chapter Twenty-Two

"Do you love me? Do you, Surfer Girl..."

-The Beach Boys.

After the auditions Dale and I returned to Michigan but with a real spring in our step. Starting the following October we had six months of work in Florida! Oh my God I couldn't believe it. I was finally out of my long depression! Days grew lush and languid like one long Brian Wilson song as I bathed in the knowledge that my time in the cold and misery was finally coming to an end. October first, we would open at Philthy Phil's in Florida. It was time for me to finally close the door on the life that I had been so used to for so long.

"You're coming back right?" Patrons would ask as our time at the Dearborn Tavern drew to a close.

"I don't think so, I'm sorry," I said but really I wasn't. I was on fire!

Before I left town, there was one more door I needed to close. All of my life, I had thought of my hometown as Kingsville. I had lived in Leamington too, in early childhood, but my teen memories, hanging with Corey, the Magnificent Six, forming bands, falling in love, would be tied forever to that cozy little town by the lake. I had loved her like a captain loves a ship.

Back in the day, it had almost seemed to me, that I had the keys to the city. Everyone had greeted me then, even the mayor! But years later as I'd wandered the sidewalks, I would rarely be recognized as I in turn would search unsuccessfully for a familiar face. This was something I could never get used to. I had entertained a fantasy about a place where they would raise me up onto their shoulders and parade me, 'ticker-tape' style, through the town, to the delighted cheers of the adoring throng. Sure it was silly. With each visit over the years it became more and more apparent that most people had simply moved away, just as I had. There was hardly anyone left that *would* remember me.

The Kingsville High School 80-year reunion would put everything in perspective. It was something the town's folk had been preparing for, for several years. 80 years of students, as many as five thousand, would be descending on the small burg for a good old fashioned 3-day-visit. At last I would get to see all the kids I remembered, and they would remember me, and everything would be all right again. I had hoped they would ask me to perform but as the time grew near, no invitation was forthcoming. With only a week to go before the event, and almost as an after thought, the call finally came. The committee had apparently succumbed to the will of an old classmate of mine who thought it would be a good idea to have me play there.

How flattering.

To me, it felt the same as back in the day when Corey's mom would reluctantly have to invite me to stay for dinner, only because, the uncomfortable option was, to tell me to go home.

No matter. I truly had wanted to give something back to my past and had nothing but myself to give. I charged nothing and asked for nothing, except a small stage. In the back of my mind, I imagined all my treasured friends coming up to me on my breaks; back slapping, reminiscing, and carrying on like the old days. I had hoped some of my teachers would be there too, so I could apologize for not being the most attentive of students. It was bound to be a cleansing experience, or so I thought.

Over the many years I had always wondered if I would ever see Susan again and what I would say to her. I felt certain I could now be candid and tell her how I had fallen for her at 17, how she had inspired me for all those years, and we'd have a good laugh and talk about other stuff too. Perhaps we'd slow dance a record or two and the memories would come flooding back. Perhaps I'd lose my mind.

On opening night after setting up my gear, I strolled among hundreds of former students, all eyes searching nametags. Here and there occasional screams of recognition could be heard, as people would spot someone they hadn't seen for 40 years! Suddenly, out of the corner of my eye, I saw a familiar face over by the makeshift bar! It was Ray, Susan's cousin. I jostled my way through the milling crowd and after some small talk I asked,

"So, how's your cousin doing? Is she coming to the reunion?" Ray's expression froze,

"Oh you didn't hear?" My heart stopped.

"About six years ago she was diagnosed with *Multiple Sclerosis*. She felt too uncomfortable coming here. I thought for sure you had heard. I'm really sorry John."

Ray filled the awkward silence with chitchat but I was no longer present. I managed a cordial,

"Good to see you man," but inside, my heart couldn't have been more broken. There were no words to say. No pain so great. Although medicine had come a long way since the days of my mother, I knew first hand what Susan and her family must have been going through. I wished I could talk to her.

Try as I might to keep my spirits up after that, the whole event had lost its appeal. Only a handful of the kids I had known had showed up and they weren't the ones I had really hoped to see anyway. There were no class clowns, no Corey, Brent, or Lonnie; no Susan. Even my performance was ignored.

But what really cinched it was the following night, when the local rock band had a jam session and invited every musician and ex-musician from the area on stage at some point during the evening, but not me. All of the years of experience, my near-misses, all the records I had produced; this whole image I had of myself came crashing down in that one single moment. I was sitting there, certain I would be called upon at any moment, and as the moments ticked away, I grew older and older and certainly more embarrassed.

Somehow the event that I had thought was going to be a cathartic experience for me turned out to be such a complete disappointment, I wished with all my heart that I had never come. Now I thought of those who didn't show, as the wise ones, the strong ones; the ones who didn't need a reunion to validate them as I apparently had. As far as the musicians were concerned, after I thought about it, I realized that they just didn't remember me; it had been too long. Time marches on. Nevertheless, I would always be a Kingsville boy, no matter what.

I snuck away quietly, headed back to Michigan, turned up the Beach Boys, cracked a bottle of White Zin and cried for the last time. That night I said goodbye forever to my past and all unhappiness. After all, I was on my way to Paradise.

Printed in the United States
104192LV00003B/235/A